Tinsel and Trickery

A Christmas Novella

Penrose & Pyke Mysteries, Book 5.5

Rose Pascoe

Published by Flax Bay Books, 2023

Copyright

TINSEL AND TRICKERY
A CHRISTMAS NOVELLA

ISBN: 978-1991181374 (POD paperback)

978-1991181367 (Epub)

Publisher: Flax Bay Books, New Zealand

Cover design: Rose Pascoe
Cover images from Shutterstock, Adobe Stock and Unsplash

Contents

Contents

A Very Merry Eviction

22 December 1892 – Wellington, New Zealand

The clamour in the assembly hall made it all but impossible to conduct hearing checks on the children. Fortunately, the cause of this boy's hearing loss was plain to see. Grace Penrose removed the aural speculum from his ear and leaned close to the other ear to be heard. "Stay still, Angus. I'm going to remove a blockage from your ear."

Angus squirmed, but not enough to stop Grace from whipping out an unidentifiable small object covered in wax and grime. When she clicked her fingers behind the ear, the boy jerked and shook his head. "Ooh, I heard that, Miss."

"No wonder you were deaf on one side," Grace said. "Do you know the golden rule for taking care of your ears?"

"No, Miss Penrose."

"Never put anything smaller than an elephant in your ear."

A half-second passed as Angus digested the advice. His reply came with a gap-toothed grin. "Especially not a washcloth, eh, Miss."

"You'll go a long way with that sharp mind of yours, Angus." Grace had noticed the boy's fascination with her medical instruments. "Perhaps you could become a doctor."

Angus shook his mop of red hair. "Too much blood and guts for me. I'm going to build a submarine, like in that book by Mr Verne. Can I go now, Miss Penrose?" At her nod, the boy bolted for the door, where he paused to reconsider. "Or maybe I'll just be a baker, like my father was. Then I'll never be hungry."

Grace took a moment to clean the speculum and reflect on the pleasures of working with a group of orphans who never ceased to surprise her. She checked her pocket watch and went to find her next patient. The queue that had snaked around the edge of the hall when they'd begun their work this morning had now vanished. Not that it was easy to tell who was a patient, with the horde of children filling the hall. Durham House Orphans' Home was bursting at the seams.

Up on the stage, the choir was practising "The First Noel" for the door-to-door carolling planned for Christmas Eve. The children's reedy voices were all but drowned out by the thump of boys from the gymnastics club hurtling over the box-horse at the front of the hall and the clatter of pans from the room at the rear, where the kitchen workers were preparing the midday meal.

Squeals and laughter added to the cacophony coming from the corner by the door, where a group of older children supervised the making of Christmas decorations. A mystery donor had left box of tinsel and crêpe paper on the doorstep this morning, igniting a minor riot of over-excited children.

Across the room, the kindergarten group half-heartedly recited the alphabet with their teacher. The elderly Miss Bentwick not only taught the orphans but also took on the roles of Matron, general factotum, and Secretary of the Durham House Charitable Foundation that ran the orphans' home. Although she was usually a stern taskmistress, even Miss Bentwick could not swim against the tide of Christmas cheer. She put down her chalk and waved a dusty hand at the children to join the decorators in the corner.

To make ends meet, the large hall attached to the orphans' home was put to a wide variety of uses. In addition to being the dining hall and classroom for the children, space in the hall was let to local clubs, such as the gymnastics team, and other charitable groups, including a soup kitchen. The medical team had set up in a small side room, hemmed in by broken chairs, tins of corned beef, a pile of thin blankets and a box of rainy-day games. Not ideal, but sharing the ever-increasing rent was the only option, with each group struggling to survive on charitable donations.

"Quiet today," said a voice behind Grace. "I expect the orphans are too excited by Christmas preparations to attend their health checks." Her father, Doctor George Penrose, was both a patron of the charitable foundation and a volunteer for the free community medical service. Indeed, Grace's grandfather, the first Doctor George Penrose, had set up the free service when he had first arrived in New Zealand half a century ago. Grace was proud to follow in their footsteps. The three generations looked alike too, with dark hair and a slim build.

Grace waited for a train to pass, its steam whistle at full blast and the rattle of wheels on the nearby tracks shaking the foundations so hard she had to brace herself. "If this is quiet, I'll never complain about Dunedin hospital again."

Grace Penrose was a third-year medical student at Otago Medical School in Dunedin – the first woman in the country to train to become a doctor. The students undertook practical training over the summer holidays. This year, her father had arranged for Grace to join his community medical team for the month leading up to Christmas, so she could spend the festive season in her home town of Wellington. Today was her last official day at the free clinic.

She checked her pocket watch surreptitiously for the tenth time.

"You are free to go, Grace," her father said. "I know you want to be in good time to meet the steamer. I can manage here."

"I can stay another half hour." Grace was eager to meet her fiancé, Charlie Pyke, off the steamer from Christchurch, but waiting at the dock wouldn't make the ship arrive any sooner, no matter how much she wished it.

She touched the chain around her neck, which kept her engagement ring safe during work hours, and allowed herself a moment to imagine their reunion after a month apart. Charlie was travelling up from

Dunedin to spend his first Christmas with Grace's family. She had tried to warn him about what the Penrose family was like when they gathered to celebrate Christmas, but he had brushed it off. As a broad-shouldered former policeman and now a private detective, Charlie reckoned there wasn't much he couldn't handle. How little he knew.

"What the blue bleeding barnacles is this?" The bellow came from the kitchen, accompanied by the clatter of a dropped pot lid.

A thin man in cracked spectacles, wearing a neatly pressed but well-worn suit, emerged from the kitchen at a brisk trot, looking over his shoulder. Two burly men followed close behind, one with a foot-long carving knife still clutched in his hand, and both displaying an abundance of amateur tattoos and knife scars.

Grace didn't blame the thin man for his hasty retreat, although the two former convicts who ran the soup kitchen were now reformed. They were known only as Reaper and Filch. Grace didn't care to ask why, but she was sure their current names were not the ones their doting mothers had cooed into their cribs.

"Oi, wait up," Reaper yelled. "Why in the name of the Seven Princes of Hell, are we being evicted from Durham House? We pay your exorbitant rent every week, don't we?"

The clamour in the hall ceased in an instant. The only sound was the tinkle of a dropped bauble and a faint rustle of tinsel from the decorating corner. One of the younger children started crying at the unaccustomed silence.

"Evicted?" The thin man fiddled nervously with his spectacles as Reaper loomed closer. The messenger appeared to be as horrified by the news as the recipient. "I was asked to deliver the letters. I didn't know you were to be evicted, I swear."

Miss Bentwick closed in on the thin man from the other direction, followed by the gym instructor and the choirmaster, with curious orphans gathering on the periphery in a tight semi-circle. Grace and her father hovered behind them.

8

"Why is the soup kitchen being evicted?" Miss Bentwick demanded to know. "If the orphans' home can be gracious enough to share their hall with the homeless and destitute in the name of charity, surely our heartless landlord can be persuaded to allow them."

"I have other letters." The thin man's voice cracked as the surrounding crowd pressed closer. He handed another letter to the leader of the gymnastics club with the tips of his fingers, as if touching the news caused him physical pain.

The gym instructor tore the envelope open and read the letter with disbelief, which quickly turned to anger. "Durham House is to be sold? Why the dickens were we not warned?"

The choirmaster took the letter from him. "Evicted as of Christmas Eve, with less than two days' notice. I've never heard anything more despicable."

Miss Bentwick snatched up the third letter and ripped the envelope open. Her jaw thrust forward under pursed lips as she read. She turned on the thin man, who eyed her with misgiving. "You're Martha Crockett's father, aren't you?"

"Yes, ma'am," Mr Crockett replied. "You must know that I had no knowledge of the contents of these letters, or I would have refused to deliver them."

Grace knew Martha Crockett from her work as a teacher at Durham House. Martha was arriving on the same steamer as Charlie, accompanied by two more orphans, her own nephew and niece. Martha would be furious to hear of the eviction. Without the meagre pay of her teaching position, the Crockett family would sink further below the poverty line, especially with two new mouths to feed.

Miss Bentwick held up her hand for silence. With the deceptive sweetness of a teacher who was about to write "could do better" on a report card, she continued. "Pray tell me, my good man, what is the meaning of this outrage?"

9

"My employer must be acting as the agent for the sale of the property," Mr Crockett replied. "I am his clerk, but I swear he told me nothing of the sale or the eviction notices."

"Who is this scoundrel?" Reaper growled.

Mr Crockett hesitated, but the sight of Reaper flexing his biceps was too much for the poor man. "Mr Spragg, from Marton & Spragg Land Agents. You must not blame him, as he will be acting on behalf of the owner."

"I don't care if he is acting for Old St Nick himself, I'm off to give this Spragg a piece of my mind," Reaper said. "Who's with me?"

Mr Crockett gulped. "He's ... he's out of town."

"This is intolerable," Miss Bentwick snapped. "Mr Crockett, you will tell your employer that Durham House will be sold over my dead body." She paused to ensure the weight of her words had impressed him. "Better yet, tell Mr Spragg it will be sold over his own dead body. Where are the orphans to go, I ask you, with the sacred holiday upon us and scarcely a moment's notice? Are we to sleep on the street and beg for crumbs, while your Mr Spragg hogs into his festive feast?"

"Yes, ma'am. I'm very sorry, truly I am. I shall be sure to inform Mr Spragg of your views when he returns tomorrow afternoon." With that, Mr Crockett made a break for the door.

"Tomorrow afternoon? But that only leaves us a day before Durham House is sold," Miss Bentwick shouted after the messenger's retreating back. "Stop! I have more questions!"

Mr Crockett never made it to the door. The group leading the decoration-making sensed trouble and sprang into action. One didn't survive being an orphan without quick wits and a gallon of pluck.

"We'll get 'im," the tallest child yelled. After a brief tussle, during which wild cries of childish triumph drowned out Mr Crockett's protests, the circle of orphans stepped aside, revealing a startled land agent's clerk loosely trussed in tinsel.

"Children, untie that man immediately! How many times do I have to tell you – we are not savages." Miss Bentwick strode across the hall with an expression that veered between outrage and long-suffering resignation.

The gym instructor sprinted past her and helped to unravel the captive. "Our profound apologies, Mr Crockett. We know it's not your fault. Never blame the messenger, eh?"

Mr Crockett did not wait for further apologies. He tipped his hat to the gym instructor and scuttled out the door.

After sending the children back to their tasks with a half-hearted reprimand, Miss Bentwick formed a huddle with the gym instructor, the choirmaster, and the two men from the soup kitchen.

Grace and her father had exchanged glances at the unwelcome news that Marton & Spragg Land Agents were behind the sale. Grace's brother worked for that business. Jake, who had teased and tormented Grace through childhood, was the most annoying of her five brothers. On a good day, Grace would have admitted that she had tormented Jake right back, but today was not a good day.

"Jake has some explaining to do." Doctor Penrose was not a man prone to anger, but his clenched jaw did not bode well for his second son. "The rest of the health checks will have to wait."

Grace held her father back with a hand on his arm. "Marton & Spragg's office is on the way home from the docks. Why don't you leave Jake to me while you finish the health checks?"

Her father cast her a glance that questioned the wisdom of setting a fuming mad Grace on her brother, but he nodded nevertheless. "Go easy on your brother, Grace. Simply ask Jake what he knows of the matter. Perhaps it is a mistake."

Grace went to offer her services to Miss Bentwick. After a rapid and not altogether harmonious discussion, Reaper's instinct to take action was subdued and Grace's proposal to investigate the situation was accepted.

Grace wasted no further time. She gathered her satchel and left. Brother Jake and his employer were about to learn that the Christmas message of peace and goodwill to all men ought to apply to orphaned children and destitute adults, as well as to the land agents and owners who would be sitting down to stuffed goose and all the trimmings in three days' time.

But first, Grace had a fiancé to meet. After a month apart, with every single hour counted until Charlie arrived for Christmas, she could not bear to wait a minute longer to see him.

Grace took her sapphire and diamond engagement ring from the chain around her neck and slid it onto her finger. She noted with satisfaction that the ring had already formed a groove in her flesh after two months of wear.

Reluctantly, she pulled a glove over the ring. The headmistress at her school had impressed upon all the girls the vital importance of wearing their gloves at all times outside their homes. One must not expose one's fingers in public, after all, in case a sensitive gentleman should see them and swoon. Personally, Grace thought such gentlemen should be kept behind locked doors, preferably doing something useful, such as tackling boring household chores.

Festive Greetings

Grace arrived at the wharf as the steamer from Christchurch docked. The vessel loomed above her, streaming a tattered banner of grey smoke in the brisk breeze. She clamped her hat tighter against her head and leaned into the buffeting wind. Having grown up in Wellington, Grace used the term "brisk breeze" to describe any wind she could stand more-or-less upright in.

The breeze was thick with the heat of a summer's day – far warmer than the norm in the southern city of Dunedin, where she now resided. Printers of Christmas cards, with their illustrations of snow-covered trees and sleighs, doggedly refused to accept that the festive season fell during summer in the Southern Hemisphere. The local British immigrants seemed content to be party to this self-deception.

Grace was happy to be back in her home city. Christmas in Dunedin was a subdued affair, because of the preponderance of Scottish settlers, who preferred to celebrate Hogmanay. Indeed, many southern folk considered it ungodly to indulge in Christmas trees, decorations, feasting and gift-giving. In contrast, Grace's family embraced the Victorian enthusiasm for celebrating Christmas, melding English festivities with the best of French traditions, thanks to the influence of Grace's beloved grandmother. Although Grandma Penrose had passed away a decade ago, her feisty exuberance lived on in Grace's heart.

Grace scanned the faces on the ship's deck eagerly, searching for Charlie Pyke. With Christmas only days away, the steamer was packed to the gunwales.

The first straggle of passengers trudged down the gangplank, wielding carpetbags, valises and children with equal lack of care. A rough trip, Grace surmised, from the pea-soup hue of their faces and sagging eyelids. When they reached the bottom of the gangplank, the passengers' expressions transformed from misery to delight, as the crowd parted to allow cherished reunions between the arrivals and waiting family and friends. Hugs and tears mostly, with the occasional gruff greeting and cursory handshake.

The straggle turned into a river of disembarking passengers. Grace craned her neck and stood on tiptoes, but her fiancé was not amongst the throng. Charlie Pyke was a hard man to miss, being six feet tall and pleasing to the eye. In fact, Charlie was pleasing to all five senses, and a few others as yet unnamed, but Grace kept that to herself.

Finally, she glimpsed a gleeful lad, who floated along above head height, forming a living necklace around the beast of burden whose shoulders held him up. The crowd cleared a little, allowing her to see the man underneath. He carried his own canvas bag slung across his broad back and another two bags in his hands. Grace couldn't see the man's face, because of the small valise the boy was clutching at head height, but she knew that purposeful stride.

Martha Crockett, the teacher from Durham House, hurried after Charlie, carrying a carpetbag in each hand and shepherding a small girl in front of her. Grace had volunteered Charlie as an escort to help Martha bring the two orphans to Wellington, after the relatives who escorted her down to Christchurch could not accompany her on the return journey with the children.

Martha was one of life's cheerful souls, who soldiered on with a sunny smile, no matter the odds. Today, she looked exhausted. Her bouncy blonde curls hung limp against her cheek as the group came to a halt to one side of the stream of travellers.

Grace ran towards them, ignoring the bumps of baggage and elbows as she pushed through the crowd. "Charlie," she yelled, waving her arms with unladylike exuberance.

Martha was prising the boy off Charlie's shoulders when Grace reached them. Martha turned to greet her. "Grace, your fiancé has been a godsend. I couldn't have managed without him."

Charlie dropped the baggage and enveloped Grace in his arms, swinging her off the ground in his excitement. "Grace, how I've missed you." He squeezed her as if he hadn't seen her in months.

"I missed you too, Charlie," Grace murmured, when she could breathe again. "Maybe you could put me down, since we are in company?" She said it for the sake of decorum, but somehow she couldn't quite manage to unlock her arms from around his neck.

Charlie glanced at the giggling children and let Grace down. "Grace, may I introduce Miss Crockett's niece, Eva, aged eight, and her nephew, Tom, aged six. Children, this is Miss Penrose, my fiancée."

"Six years and ten months," Tom corrected in a small voice from behind Charlie's leg, which he gripped with a monkey's strength.

Charlie whispered in the boy's ear, before unwrapping his arms and disappearing into the crowd. Eva stepped between Grace and her brother protectively, but she curtsied politely as well. Tom withdrew behind his sister, but not before Grace noticed he was dragging one foot awkwardly.

"Pleased to meet you, Miss Eva." Grace crouched down to greet them, shaking Eva's hand. She had to reach around the girl to shake the boy's hand. "You've had a long journey, Master Tom. Welcome to Wellington."

"We'll be glad to get home, won't we, children?" Martha said. "Your grandma is eager to meet you. She'll have a tasty meal waiting, you can be sure. Grandpa will be home later." Martha turned to Grace. "Will you be at Durham House tomorrow, Grace? Eva and Tom will come with me to my reading class. I wondered if you could include them in your health checks."

"Of course," Grace replied. "I will not be there, but my father will be happy to oblige."

From the way Tom moved, Grace thought it likely he had a club foot. With time and patience, the twisted limb could be partially straightened, if not fully fixed. It would have been better to treat it at an early age, but casting a club foot was a gradual process that took weeks of medical attention, possibly even tenotomy surgery and a brace. The expense of the treatment would be too much for a family of limited means, but Grace was sure her father would undertake the work at no charge. Sometimes, she wondered if he ever had time for paying patients.

As she would soon remind her brother Jake, this was exactly why it was essential to support charitable foundations that provided free medical care. Even in this age of scientific advancement, there were still people who saw impediments such as a club foot as the mark of the devil. Without medical help, Tom might be shunned all his life and kept from fulfilling his dreams.

"I want Charlie to come with us too," Tom said.

Martha squeezed his hand. "Tom Crockett, where are your manners? He is Mr Pyke to you, and he has to look after Miss Penrose now."

Tom frowned at Grace, no doubt thinking she was old enough to look after herself. But he didn't argue.

Grace's heart melted at the sight of his disappointment. "Mr Pyke will find time to stop by Durham House to see you tomorrow, Tom, if he can."

"Thank you, Miss Penrose," Tom replied, after a nudge from Martha. "Mr Pyke showed us magic tricks."

"I like the trick where he makes a coin appear from behind your ear." Grace had seen Charlie perform the trick whenever children (and adults) were in need of distraction. "Perhaps Mr Pyke can show the other children that one tomorrow."

Grace took Martha aside. "I hate to add to your burden, Martha, but I should warn you that Durham House is to be sold."

"No! What dreadful news. I haven't heard a whisper about it."

"None of us knew. You'll have to ask your father for the details, but go easy on him – he has had a tough day too."

Charlie was striding their way, waving. "I've hired you a hackney to get home." He scooped up the two squealing children and their baggage and dived through the crowd at speed.

Martha and Grace hurried after him, losing him once, before spotting him loading up a carriage. Tom sat next to the coachman, his face alight with excitement as he waved at them.

Martha waved back. "Bless your Mr Pyke. Tom and Eva have hardly spoken a word since their parents passed away. I hope they will make new friends amongst the orphans, before they start at the local school next year."

Charlie handed Martha into the carriage and waved until they were out of sight. He slung his canvas bag across his back and took Grace's arm, whispering, "Alone at last, my love." He glanced around the noisy swirl of passengers, porters, dockworkers, and carriages. "Although not as alone as I would like. Shall we go?"

Grace led the way out of the chaos of the wharf.

"I hope that the new year will bring the Crockett family good fortune," Charlie said. "It's sad to see a decent family struggling, and even harder to see two children orphaned so young. Martha said their parents died crossing a flooded river on the Canterbury plains. The aunt who took them in after the tragedy can no longer afford to keep them, hence their move to Wellington."

"How dreadful. Those poor children." Grace had seen more than her fair share of drownings while working for the police surgeon. New Zealand's wild rivers exacted a harsh toll on new settlers, although most of the deaths she saw were the result of drunks falling into smaller streams and ponds.

Grace sighed. "I'm afraid that the family fortunes are about to take yet another turn for the worse. Martha teaches the orphans at Durham House, which is to be sold. All the charitable groups who use the hall were served with eviction notices this morning, effective from Christmas Eve. It won't be easy for so many groups to find a new place to pursue their good works, let alone a new house for the orphans to live in."

"What heartless scoundrel would evict orphans at Christmas?" Charlie asked.

"The land agent my brother Jake works for, that's who. Mr Spragg of Marton & Spragg." In Grace's opinion, Spragg deserved to be flogged with spiky holly branches for the cold-hearted eviction, even if he was only acting on behalf of the owner. Holly would be the least of his torments if Reaper and Filch had their way. The men from the soup kitchen might have left behind their criminal pasts, but they were not men who shied away from a fight when their backs were against a wall.

"Can you find your own way to my parents' house, Charlie? I'm going to have stern words with Jake. I'm sorry to abandon you as soon as you arrive, but this cannot wait."

Charlie tightened his grip on her arm. "I'd rather go with you. Let's give Jake a chance to explain before we bring out the thumbscrews. Your brother might have nothing to do with the sale."

"A fair point, but he must be able to find out." Grace paused on a corner to get her bearings. She turned down a side-street, heading into the heart of the city. "Martha Crockett's father is the clerk at Marton & Spragg and he knew nothing about the sale. Spragg ordered Mr Crockett to deliver the letters without warning the poor man he was delivering eviction notices to the place his daughter worked."

Charlie lengthened his stride to keep up with her fast pace. "Heartless, but also odd. One might expect the clerk to have drawn up the letters and sale documents. I have to wonder why Mr Spragg did it himself without informing his clerk."

Grace perked up. She could always rely on Charlie to tackle a crisis logically. "Are you thinking the sale might be underhand or illegal? Perhaps we can stop it going ahead."

"Maybe, but we shouldn't jump to conclusions without evidence. Mr Crockett might have had time off on the day the papers were drawn up, perhaps to prepare for the arrival of his orphaned grandchildren."

Grace snorted. "Unlikely. From what Martha and Jake say about Mr Spragg, he wouldn't allow them time off for anything short of being on their deathbeds. Even then, he'd probably simply give them their notice rather than a day of leave. Martha says the office is so cold in winter that her father wears more layers of clothes inside than outside. They have a fireplace, but the coal is strictly rationed."

"Perhaps business is not good and they have to trim their expenses?"

"Charlie, you see the best in everyone. You may be right, but I believe they sell a good many properties and manage the lease on many others. I've never met Spragg, but he sounds like a horrible miser." Grace darted across the street without looking.

"Careful, Grace," Charlie pulled her out of the way of a pair of horses, whose riders were too engrossed in their conversation to notice a distracted pedestrian. "What of Mr Marton?"

"Marton & Spragg was founded by the current Mr Spragg's father and his friend, Mr Marton, who are both now deceased. Jake was happy there when he first started, as the founding owners of the business treated him well and took the time to train him. Mr Marton passed away a couple of years ago, I believe. Young Mr Spragg took over when his father died last year. I haven't seen Jake since then, but my mother's letters suggest his current position is not a happy one."

Grace turned the corner into the main street, Lambton Quay, where afternoon strollers shared the pavement with hawkers and signboards. The air became thick with the smell and sound of a steady stream of

19

horse-drawn vehicles of all shapes and sizes. Grace had only visited Jake at work once, over a year ago, while old Mr Spragg had still been in charge. She recalled walking part way along Lambton Quay, before turning left down another street and left again into a narrow lane. The question was, which one?

After one wrong turn, Grace found the right street, but the first lane she tried came to a dead end at a blank brick wall. The only inhabitants were pigeons and rats. The wall leaned ominously and was bisected by a long crack, presumably a relic of the massive earthquake that had devastated Wellington mid-century.

Grace squeezed Charlie's arm. "Sorry, my love, this isn't the charming view of Wellington I wanted to share with you on your Christmas holiday."

"The lane may not be pretty, but it has one redeeming feature. We are alone at last. I hated to be apart from you for so long." Charlie seized the opportunity to secure a lingering kiss.

Grace sank into his embrace, only pulling away when she ran out of air. She smoothed his jet-black hair back into place and retrieved his hat from the ground. "Let's find out about the property sale and report back to Durham House as quickly as we can, so we will be free to spend time together without distractions. We could walk home through the Botanical Gardens. As children, we used to roam wild there, finding many a secluded nook to hide away from the world."

"Sounds heavenly," Charlie murmured. "We must spend time with your family too. I expect your mother wishes to discuss the arrangements for our wedding next month."

"I've had nearly a month of my mother's enthusiasm already," Grace said. "I told her we wanted a simple wedding. Your Aunt Lily is making my gown, your mother is doing the flowers, the local ladies are providing the food, the date has been secured at St Andrew's and the banns have been read. Honestly, what more needs to be done?" Grace paused momentarily before answering her own question. "Orders of service, instructing the vicar, specifications for the wedding meal, wine for the toast, checking who can and cannot come, choosing who will sit where based on long-ago family rifts, thank you cards for gifts, music choices … the list of tasks is never-ending. All I want is for you to turn up and say 'I do'."

"You may be assured of that."

They returned to the street and turned the next corner into a more salubrious lane, spotting a sign above a door proclaiming "Marton & Spragg, Land Agents" in gold lettering.

Charlie paused outside. "Your mother only has one daughter, Grace. Let her enjoy the thrill of the only wedding you will ever have. Besides, I want to make the most of experiencing a large and harmonious family Christmas."

Harmonious? Charlie was an only child, so Grace knew he had no idea what he truly faced. The arguments over the quantity of tinsel to apply to the Christmas tree and whose turn it was to place the star on top. The disagreement over who got the legs of the roast goose and the last slice of yule log, followed by the squabbling over whose turn it was to help with the washing up. And then there was the rigorous adherence to arcane Penrose family traditions, including – but not limited to – old family jokes, foolish pranks, present shaking, and the reading of Charles Dickens' Christmas story.

"I'm afraid my family can be rather overwhelming at Christmas," Grace ventured, clutching his arm tightly, in case her admission caused him to run. Not that it was likely. Charlie Pyke had faced knife-wielding madmen, lunatics, anarchists, arsonists and more. The Penrose family was no worse than any of these, individually, at least.

"I've met all your family, except Luke," Charlie said, with the equanimity of a man who had never experienced her family *en masse* during the festive season. "Your parents were always most welcoming to me when I lived in Wellington, although it's true that they may not have viewed me as a future son-in-law back then. I count your brother

George as a friend. As for your other brothers, they may be a little boisterous, but all in good fun."

Grace had five brothers, of whom four would be there for Christmas. Luke was working in the Pacific Islands, rebuilding homes after a devastating cyclone season. Her beloved older brother, George, had inherited the sweet nature of their mother, but the other three brothers were as lively as a barrel of monkeys and twice as mischievous.

"Boisterous is putting it mildly, Charlie. The twins are uncivilised little imps. As for my brother Jake, you must always be on guard or he will catch you out with his childish pranks. Naturally, this being the first time we have visited together, we must also expect a great deal of teasing over your desire to marry me. Jake has been a pain in the *gluteus maximus* my whole life. I'll throttle him if he had anything to do with selling Durham House."

Charlie pushed open the door of the land agency. "Perhaps it might be best if I question Jake."

Marton & Spragg

The bell hanging on the back of the door gave an apologetic little tinkle as they entered. A short passage took them to an office at the rear of the building, which was so gloomy that at first glance Charlie doubted anyone was present. Wellington city had embraced electric street lighting over the past three years, but it hadn't yet penetrated the premises of Marton & Spragg. Nor was there a single sign that the festive season was upon them – not a sprig of holly, not a hint of tinsel, and certainly no bright star lighting the way.

From behind a desk piled with papers, a thin, stooped man rose, straightening cracked spectacles on a narrow nose. "Good afternoon, sir. I am Mr Crockett, Mr Spragg's clerk. Mr Spragg is out of town today, but Mr Penrose or I would be pleased to assist you."

Charlie had assumed Martha Crockett's father would be about the same age as Grace's father, but this man looked worn down by the grind of sand through the hourglass, in contrast to the vibrant youthfulness of Doctor Penrose. The man's suit did nothing to dispel the impression, as the style had been out of fashion long before Charlie's first constable's uniform had been thrown in his direction by an uncaring quartermaster.

"Miss Grace Penrose is here to see her brother," Charlie said. "I am her fiancé, Mr Charlie Pyke."

Mr Crockett peered over his spectacles. "Miss Penrose from the medical team? My daughter, Martha, has told me of your good works. And Mr Pyke, you must be the gentleman who assisted Martha in bringing my grandchildren to Wellington. They have arrived safely, I trust?"

"Indeed, sir. Eva and Tom are well, but tired after a long journey. It was my pleasure to escort them. They are as delightful a pair of youngsters as I have ever met."

Mr Crockett grasped Charlie's hand and pumped it. "I cannot tell you how grateful I am to you for accompanying them on the journey. Martha has never been out of Wellington before and thus was rightly nervous of travelling such a distance." The clerk turned to call for his colleague. "Mr Penrose, your sister is here to see you."

"Grace?" A head popped up on the far side of the room beyond a low partition.

Charlie had met Jake Penrose before, but even if he hadn't, the man's lean build, dark hair, and piercing blue eyes would have identified him as a Penrose. Jake bounded over to greet them with the eagerness of a puppy that has been indoors for too long.

Jake shook Charlie's hand. "Ah, the martyr has arrived. Mr Crockett, you see before you the bravest man in New Zealand – the man who has plighted his troth to my rebellious sister Grace. My commiserations, Charlie. I hope you don't harbour any delusions of changing my sister into a meek and obedient servant to your every need."

"Fortunately, I love Grace the way she is," Charlie replied. "Clever, determined, kind, and courageous. Perfect in every way."

Jake slapped him on the back. "By Jove, you really are smitten. Don't scowl at me, sister dearest. You know I am only teasing. I wish you both the greatest of happiness. I must say, it was kind of you to visit me at work instead of waiting until this evening."

Grace rounded on her brother. "Do not think it was out of the goodness of my heart, Jake Penrose. We want to know how the devil Marton & Spragg came to be evicting the orphans from Durham House onto the street on Christmas Eve. I warn you, brother, I shall never forgive you if you had anything to do with it."

24

Jake backed away. "Whoa there, Grace. Calm down. I fear you have your facts in a tangle. Marton & Spragg are the leasing agents for Durham House. I can assure you that there is no intention to evict the current tenants, as far as I am aware."

Mr Crockett cleared his throat. "I regret to say, Mr Penrose, that your sister is correct. Mr Spragg asked me to deliver letters to the tenants this morning. I assumed the letters were about the rent for the coming year, but they were eviction notices. I didn't believe it myself, sir. I decided not to share the news with you until I had spoken to Mr Spragg, because I was sure the letters must have been drafted in error."

"I knew nothing of this," Jake said. "Did you not prepare the eviction notice, Mr Crockett?"

"No. Mr Spragg must have seen to it himself."

"Do you know who the new tenants are?" Jake asked.

"The property is to be sold, Mr Penrose, according to the letter to the tenants. I did not draft the sale documents either."

Jake took a set of keys from his pocket and unlocked the door to one of two rooms off the main office. The name of the previous partner, Mr Marton, was still on the door. The room was set up with chairs, presumably for client meetings, with a row of wooden filing drawers along the side of the room. Charlie wondered why Jake and Mr Crockett did not work in this room, which was lighter and more spacious than the gloomy room they currently worked in.

Jake found the file for Durham House and leafed through it. "The file contains only the usual tenancy information. There is nothing to indicate the building has been or will be sold. There now, I told you the eviction notice must be a mistake."

"If Mr Spragg handled the sale personally, perhaps the file is in his office," Grace suggested. "We could –"

Jake closed the filing drawer with more force than was strictly necessary. "No, Grace, absolutely not. I will not search Mr Spragg's office. He would boot me out on the street without notice if he caught me interfering in his private business dealings."

"But Jake," Grace pleaded, "you must see that the reputation of Marton & Spragg – and thus your own reputation – will be tarnished by the cruel eviction of orphans at Christmas."

"No, Grace, I do not. If Durham House is to be sold, Mr Spragg will be acting on the orders of the owner of the property. If Mr Spragg does not wish his employees to know of the sale, that is his decision. As it happens, I cannot enter his office anyway, as I do not have a key."

Mr Crockett appeared in the doorway. "I have a spare key for Mr Spragg's office, to be used only if he forgets to bring his own key or if an urgent matter arises. I believe your sister is correct, Mr Penrose. This qualifies as a matter of urgency."

Grace plucked the key from Mr Crockett's hand before he changed his mind. She had unlocked Mr Spragg's office before Jake disentangled himself from Charlie, who had collided with Jake as they both rushed after her to the door. From the twinkle in Charlie's eye, the collision was no accident.

"Don't touch anything, Grace," Jake ordered. "I will conduct the search."

Grace held up her hands and went to stand by the window, out of Jake's way.

No searching was required, as the Durham House file was on Mr Spragg's desk. Jake flicked through the documents, his expression going from grim to grimmer. "Mr Crockett is correct. The file contains the purchaser's copy of the sale deeds and property information. Durham House has been sold, with the sale taking effect on Christmas Eve. There is nothing we can do, as the documents have been signed. I presume the owner was desperate to sell in haste."

Grace joined her brother by the desk, reaching out her hand for the file. "I need to check the name of the owner of Durham House."

Jake clutched the file to his chest. "Grace, these documents are confidential. I cannot let you stick your inquisitive nose into Mr Spragg's business, nor that of his clients."

Grace kept her hand extended, but Jake did not budge. "Please, Jake. All I want is to know is who the seller and buyer are, so we can have a quiet word with them. They must see that this sale cannot go ahead without a fair period of notice to the orphans' home."

Jake didn't waver. "I agree it is uncharitable, Grace, but what can I do? Mr Spragg is out of town and the buyer and seller have agreed to the sale, as is their right. That is the reality of business." Jake put the documents back on the desk in the exact position he had found them and ushered them out of the office.

"We have to do something, Jake," Grace persisted. "Could we not talk to Mr Spragg? If the purchaser has not yet received his copy of the sale deeds, perhaps we can stop the sale?"

Jake locked the door behind him. "No, Grace. I would lose my position here if you interfere when you have no right to do so."

"Mr Spragg is due back tomorrow afternoon," Mr Crockett said. "He intends to return around three o'clock, to finish up the last matters of business before the Christmas holiday."

"Is he often out of town?" Charlie asked.

"I am not aware of the nature of any dealings outside of Wellington," Jake replied, "but Mr Spragg seems to be away quite often. I don't presume to ask Mr Spragg his business, when he is unwilling to talk of it."

While Grace had been tackling her brother, Charlie had taken stock of the premises of Marton & Spragg, Land Agents. The fittings were old, as were the furnishings, while the floor was scratched and unpolished. Although it was summer, the room was chilly because of its position in the shade of the surrounding taller buildings, yet the fire remained unlit and the coal scuttle was empty.

"Might one assume from the state of this place that the business is not thriving?" Charlie ventured.

Jake sighed. "I don't know. As I have made clear, Mr Spragg is a gentleman who values his privacy."

Grace waved her hand around. "Use your initiative, Jake. Search the files and accounts to find out the state of affairs. Visit his home to see if he lives in poverty or wealth."

"Grace! I cannot search through confidential files that I have no legitimate cause to inspect. And I most certainly would not breach the privacy of my employer's residence."

Fortunately, Mr Crockett was not so reticent. "Mr Spragg lives in a grand home on Tinakori Road, Miss Penrose, inherited from his father. The business was a great success in old Mr Spragg's day, but perhaps young Mr Spragg has fallen on hard times of late." Mr Crockett caught the black look Jake sent him and retreated to his desk. "Excuse me, I must get back to my work."

Grace took her brother aside. "Why do you work for a man like Spragg, Jake?"

A cloud darkened Jake's face, as if he was not sure himself. "Mr Spragg Senior and Mr Marton were very good to me, when I first joined the agency with nothing to recommend me but my eagerness to learn. I feel I owe them my loyalty. Truth be told, I am not sure I would get a good reference from the younger Mr Spragg if I left. There aren't many available openings for a man of my experience." Jake dropped his voice to a whisper. "I am saving so I can start a business of my own, but Spragg pays a pittance. When I asked for a raise, he said he could not afford to pay a higher wage."

Grace kept her voice low as well. "Martha Crockett says Spragg treats her father badly too. If she loses her position at Durham House, the family will struggle to survive. Martha is a fine woman, Jake. I should not care to see her brought low by this infamous sale of the orphans' home."

A soft smile turned Jake's lips up at the ends. "Miss Crockett comes in regularly to deliver meals to her father, who works long hours. She's a lovely lady, both in her nature and her countenance. Any school would be grateful to have her if she loses her position. However, I agree with you, Grace. I will have stern words with Mr Spragg as soon as he comes in tomorrow, to see if we cannot delay the sale until the orphans' home has time to find new premises. It is the best I can do, I am afraid."

Charlie could see that they would achieve nothing more here. The long journey from Dunedin to Wellington caught up with him all of a sudden, leaving him eager to sink into a comfortable chair. "In that case, we'll leave it in your hands, Jake."

They left Marton & Spragg in silence.

Charlie doubted they could persuade Spragg to delay the sale. If he treated his employees in a miserly and heartless manner, he would likely care little for orphans. Besides, as Jake had said, it was a matter between buyer and seller, with Spragg only acting as the agent. Unless the purchase terms had been forced upon either party by unscrupulous means, there seemed little chance that the sale could be prevented.

If Spragg refused to help, their only other option was to persuade Jake Penrose to reveal the parties to the sale, and quickly, so they could talk to them directly and convince them to accept a delay. Charlie could think of more enjoyable ways to spend the time on his much-anticipated visit to the Penrose family. He had envisaged secluded walks with Grace and lively dinners in her family home, surrounded by her loved ones and all the trappings of the festive season.

"You look exhausted, Charlie," Grace said. "I have to call in to Durham House on the way home, to pass on the bad news that the eviction notice is not a mistake. Why don't you go straight home?"

The offer was tempting, but Grace deserved his support and Charlie couldn't bear to be parted from her. "We'll go together."

Durham House was only a short detour from their route home. As they entered, Grace pointed out the tinsel discarded in a heap around the bottom of the tree. "It would seem the orphans have abandoned all hope of a merry Christmas. I wish I had better news to impart."

The matron spotted them and hurried over. Grace promised Miss Bentwick that she would do all in her power to delay the sale, but her promise rang hollow, even to Charlie's sympathetic ear. Miss Bentwick thanked Grace with polite resignation. Charlie asked her whether she knew the owner, but the matron had only had dealings with the agent who leased the property, Mr Spragg.

Doctor Penrose was tidying up after completing the health checks. "Charlie, good to have you back in Wellington. Welcome to the Penrose family." He extended his hand, but changed his mind and embraced Charlie instead. "I can't tell you how delighted my wife and I are that you asked Grace to marry you. Mrs Penrose was particularly touched that you asked for her consent as well as mine."

The warmth of Doctor Penrose's greeting reassured Charlie that he was truly welcome as a son-in-law. Having not seen Grace's family since their relationship moved beyond friendship, it put his mind at ease. "The pleasure is all mine, Doctor Penrose. I am honoured that Grace accepted my proposal and you both gave your consent."

"Grace would never have forgiven us if we hadn't approved the match, while we would never have forgiven her if she had refused your proposal. Not that there was any doubt. Grace has been cavorting around like a debutante at her first ball, fluttering her ring finger in front of everyone from the milkman to the ladies in her mother's whist group."

"Wild exaggeration," Grace grumbled, although she couldn't help glancing at her ring finger again. "Everybody begged to see my beautiful ring. It would have been rude not to show them."

Doctor Penrose arched an eyebrow. "Everybody? Do I not recall your brother Jake vowing to throw the ring into the harbour if you waved it in front of his face one more time?"

Grace sniffed. "Jake is so miserable himself, he cannot bear to see others happy."

Doctor Penrose ignored Grace's comment. "To see one's daughter happy is a fine thing, Charlie, as I hope you will find out one day. I hate to bring up less joyful matters, but what news of the sale of Durham House?"

"Confirmed, unfortunately," Charlie said. "But Jake knew nothing of the sale or eviction notice. Mr Spragg is out of town, so we cannot see him until tomorrow afternoon."

"Bad news, indeed. The only comfort is that Jake had no hand in it. Grace, don't make that lemon-sucking face. You must be nice to your brother, for the sake of a peaceful family Christmas."

"We are not entirely out of options," Charlie hastened to say, cutting off the retort he could see forming on Grace's lips. "Although the best we can hope for is a last-minute meeting to beg for a temporary delay to the eviction."

Doctor Penrose watched on with amusement. "You two simply cannot go anywhere without being drawn into an investigation. On behalf of the orphans and all the rest of us who rely on Durham House, I thank you."

"We'll do our best, but we don't want to get your hopes up," Grace said. "In all likelihood, there will be nothing we can do to stop the sale proceeding. Are you ready to come home, Father?"

"Give me two minutes."

"Perfect. Charlie will help you, while I tell Reaper the news."

Charlie watched Grace impart the bad news to the muscle-bound ex-convict who ran the soup kitchen. Reaper was far from happy. Charlie wouldn't want to be in Spragg's shoes if the soup man took it into his head to convey his displeasure in person.

Tinsel And Turmoil

Grace was looking forward to a peaceful evening, imagining her family brimming with good cheer as they welcomed Charlie to their home for the first time as her betrothed. He would be staying at her Aunt Sophie's house in the interests of propriety, but there was no time to go there now, as they were running late.

The noise hit Grace square in both eardrums when she opened the front door of her family home. From the sound of it, her twin sixteen-year-old brothers were having a disagreement. The uninitiated always assumed that identical twins acted as a single harmonious entity. In reality, their moments of brotherly camaraderie alternated with fierce rivalry. If the meek inherited the earth, Peter and Paul would not be among them.

Grace opened the drawing room to find the nativity scene knocked askew, the Christmas tree on the floor, and the twins tussling in a tangle of tinsel, blaming each other for the mess. Grace had had more than enough drama for one day. She left the situation in her father's capable hands and went to the kitchen to find her mother.

The maid spared Grace no more than a distraught glance as she mopped up spilled peas and water from the floor. Another liquid of an ominously deep red colour had pooled under the table. The housekeeper-cook scowled as she flapped away tendrils of smoke curling from the coal range.

Grace made a hasty retreat upstairs to tap on her parents' bedroom door. When there was no answer, she gestured for Charlie to wait in the hall while she went in. Mrs Penrose was lying on her bed with a wet cloth over her face and her pillow clasped around her ears.

"Mama? Are you ill?"

"Grace, darling? Is that the time?" Mrs Penrose rose and straightened her gown. "One of those days, I'm afraid. I needed a moment to regain my sanity."

"What happened?"

"Nothing serious." Mrs Penrose sat at her dressing table, adjusting her hair and patting powder onto flushed cheeks. "The goose the butcher delivered was underweight, the greengrocer was out of parsnips, Sarah dropped one of the good platters, the cream curdled, Paul knocked over the bowl of berries, then bumped into Peter, who overturned the peas ... well, you get the picture. I sent the twins to read quietly in the drawing room to get them out of the way."

Grace crossed her fingers and hoped her father and brothers had restored order to the drawing room before her mother saw it. She opted for the one piece of good news instead. "Charlie is here."

"Oh, goodness – Charlie, of course. How could I have forgotten?"

Mrs Penrose pushed her chair back and hurried to the door, flinging herself at her future son-in-law as one might grasp a lifebuoy in a stormy sea. Grace understood the reaction well. How many times had Charlie's calming influence and solid dependability restored her own composure in a tight spot? Many a criminal had mistaken him for a policeman who relied on brawn over brain, but Charlie's superficial calm disguised a sharp intellect and quick reflexes, especially when Grace was in danger.

Grace's mother weighed no more than a child and hardly reached Charlie's shoulder, but she knocked him backwards in her enthusiasm. "Dearest Charlie, how delightful it is to have you here for Christmas. We were overjoyed when you proposed to Grace. The whole family is looking forward to welcoming you as one of our own."

Grace had failed to mention to Charlie that the entire Penrose clan was gathering on Christmas Day, including four dozen or so aunts, uncles, cousins and sundry others. She would have to chain herself to him or she would lose him in the crowd.

"I won't hear of you staying with Sophie," Mrs Penrose continued. "I need you here to ensure that my brood are on their best behaviour. We have a spare bedroom now that Luke is away and George has his own home. Follow me."

Grace left her fiancé to her mother's tender care and went downstairs to the drawing room to see if she could help. Miraculously, her father had the tree upright, the floor swept and the twins putting the last of the tinsel back on the tree.

As Grace entered the room, Peter and Paul stood back, side by side, gazing at the tree with angelic expressions. "Looks wonderful, boys," she said. "Your mother has had a trying day. Can you please be on your best behaviour?"

Grace didn't wait for an answer. She went to the kitchen, where order had been restored. Grace set the table in the dining room, putting out the best plates and crystal glasses for the occasion. When she returned to the drawing room, her mother was in her favourite armchair, with Peter plumping her cushion and Paul handing her the sherry her husband had wisely poured.

In Grace's absence, her brother George had arrived and was chatting amiably with Charlie. Charlie and George had formed a firm friendship from their first meeting. George, who was Grace's oldest brother, ran a successful business importing scientific and medical equipment. He had a wife and young child, who were visiting relatives this evening, while George came to welcome Charlie to the family.

The Christmas tree sparkled with tinsel, a row of Christmas cards lined the mantlepiece, and the family copy of Charles Dickens' *A Christmas Carol* sat ready on the sideboard. Grace took a seat with a deep sigh of satisfaction. The festive season spirit was alive and well. As long as nobody mentioned the Durham House debacle.

"Durham House has been sold." Doctor Penrose sank into the armchair beside his wife. "It is a travesty of justice. The orphans will be left homeless on Christmas Eve."

Mrs Penrose choked on her sherry, shedding ruby-red droplets on her gown. "How shocking. Are you sure, my dear?"

"Marton & Spragg are the agents for the sale. Jake says he knew nothing of it, but he found the documents and confirmed the sale. I suggest we not speak of it when Jake arrives, as he must be feeling terrible about the eviction."

"Not terrible enough to warrant action, I imagine." Mrs Penrose deposited her sherry glass on a side table with enough force to wobble the legs. "Well, I can tell you, my fellow members of the Durham House Charitable Foundation will not allow it. If necessary, I shall gather the ladies and we will chain ourselves to the fence to stop this outrage."

Grace's heart swelled with pride at her mother's response. "An excellent plan, Mama, but perhaps the chains can wait until after Charlie and I have investigated the sale. We aim to persuade Jake to tell us the name of the owner of Durham House, so we can call on him tomorrow morning to plead for the sale to be withdrawn or delayed. If that doesn't work, we will visit Mr Spragg tomorrow afternoon."

Mrs Penrose took up her glass again. "Can you not allow your fiancé a moment's rest, Grace, when he has travelled from afar to see us? As for you, my dear daughter, you made me a solemn promise to come shopping for fabric. If we don't purchase the satin and lace and other wedding accoutrements tomorrow, Lily won't have time to make your gown before the wedding."

"I haven't forgotten," Grace said, although she had. "We will go as planned as soon as the shops open tomorrow. Charlie can indulge in the rare pleasure of an extended sleep while we are out." By going early, Grace was sure she would still have time to visit the owner of the orphans' home at a respectable hour, as long as her mother did not become too carried away with the thrill of shopping for her daughter's wedding.

Her mother lifted her sherry glass in salute, just as Jake arrived. Jake, Grace's second oldest brother – twenty-six years old compared to her twenty-three years – still lived at home.

"Evening everyone," Jake said, in the cheerful tone of a man with nothing more than a pleasant evening on his mind. He flopped into a chair next to Charlie and George. "How splendid the drawing room looks with the Christmas tree decorated. Mother dear, you look as if you haven't moved from your chair all day. A well-earned rest for the lady of the house, I'm sure."

Grace's blood pressure rose to sphygmomanometer-bursting point, while her mother's eyes glinted daggers at her tactless son. Charlie must have seen it too, because he diverted the conversation back to George's business, dragging Jake into the discussion.

"I must show you the latest microscope we have in stock," George enthused. "I expect there would be many applications for your detective work."

"I'd be interested to see it," Charlie replied, "but we're not in a position to be purchasing any more instruments in the near future."

"Why?" Jake interrupted. "Is your detective business not making a profit?"

"Jake, it's impolite to inquire about such matters," Mrs Penrose said.

"Why, Mother? If Charlie is to marry Grace, it behoves us to know that he can support her properly."

Grace jumped up to remonstrate with her brother, but Jake waved her down. "I admire Charlie, naturally, as do we all," her brother continued, with reckless disregard for the glares around him. "I mean no disrespect. But it seems to me that attempting to start a business as untried as a private detective agency is fraught with risk. This is Grace's future we are talking of."

"Of course the detective agency will be a success," Grace declared, "and I will not listen to you spouting such foolishness, Jake Penrose. Charlie is a first-class detective, as is his partner."

Jake lounged in his chair with an annoyingly superior smirk. "So you say, Grace, but can he make a good living by offering his services in a private capacity, when we have a perfectly adequate police force to do the same work for free? You will thank me for inquiring, before you find yourself struggling to put bread on the table for your children in a year or two."

Grace bit back her annoyance, for fear of embarrassing Charlie and ruining the hitherto peaceful family gathering. In truth, although Charlie was an excellent detective, the income from the detective agency was rather erratic. The agency, which had only been established a few months ago, was the first of its kind in the country. While it was unlikely to collapse in debt if it failed, owing to the private wealth of Charlie's business partner, its success was far from assured.

Mrs Penrose sprang to her daughter's rescue. "Jake, you think far too much about money and far too little about love and the courage to follow your dreams. Besides, you need look no further than the gorgeous ring on Grace's finger to know that Charlie is making a fine success of the detective agency."

Jake looked abashed, but he could be as tenacious as a mongrel with a bone when it suited him. "One can borrow to make such purchases, Mother. I don't mean to imply that is the case. My point is that it is our duty to be sure of what fate awaits Grace."

"Fate?" Grace spluttered. "What, you mean happiness and joy? You'd do well to look for that yourself, brother, rather than criticising others for their choices. You're so darn mean, you won't even tell me who owns of Durham House, when orphans' lives are at stake."

"I warn you, Grace, do not ask me to breach business confidentiality again. I am only trying to protect you."

"If I might say something," Charlie interrupted, in the soothing voice he used for bereaved relatives, hysterical witnesses, and vicious dogs. It flowed into Grace's ear canal and through her nervous system like an intoxicating mix of morphine and honey.

"Your consideration of your sister's wellbeing is appreciated, Jake," Charlie continued. "In point of fact, I did not borrow the money to buy the ring. The agency has been profitable thus far, but you are right that it is early days. That is why we do not wish to overspend on new equipment, in order to build up our savings against any future downturn. Your sister is fully aware that she is not marrying a wealthy man, but she has agreed nevertheless. You need not doubt that I will cherish Grace and do my best for her."

"Hear, hear," Doctor Penrose said. "Let that be an end to it, as we have already given our full and unreserved consent to the match. Now that we are all here, we should toast the happy couple."

The toast, and the dinner that followed, passed peacefully. Charlie chatted to George and Doctor Penrose, while Grace was drawn into a discussion with her mother about wedding arrangements, and Jake swapped jokes and insults with the twins.

When the meal was over, Grace gathered up the dishes and dragooned the twins into helping her wash up. Although the Penrose family employed a housekeeper-cook and a maid, they also expected their children to contribute to the endless work required to keep a household operating. Clearing the table and washing up had been their job ever since the Penrose children were tall enough to reach the sink in the scullery.

Misbehaviour had been punished in a similarly practical manner. Punishments were meted out on a sliding scale, from assisting with the dusting for minor disobedience, to the onerous graft of cleaning and polishing the coal stove for major transgressions. Paul and Jake had become dab hands with the stove blacking over the years. Grace had mostly kept her hands clean, albeit largely by stealth rather than exemplary behaviour. Peter was usually too busy reading books to merit punishments, while George had always been well behaved by nature, but helped the others anyway.

Grace was making a start on the pile of dishes and pans when Jake came in with the last items for washing.

"My apologies for calling your fiancé's financial circumstances into question, Grace. I meant no disrespect to his character. I haven't always been the best of brothers, but I do care about you."

"I know, Jake. Let's say no more of it. If you want to apologise, you could wash this heap of dirty dishes for me."

Jake backed away so quickly he bumped into the windowsill. "I'll leave you to it, dear sister. I have to get the last of the Christmas decorations out of the closet. What do you say, boys? Shall we put Grandma's ornaments on the Christmas tree once you've finished the dishes?"

The twins set to their task of drying dishes with crystal-threatening eagerness, but it still took them a long time to work through the pile. When they were finished, Grace and the twins gathered the rest of the family, who were still sitting around the table in the dining room, and ushered them into the drawing room. They found Jake standing by the tree, holding a box of ornaments in his hands, ready for another of the Penrose Christmas rituals.

Mrs Penrose took a seat on the sofa, beckoning Charlie over. "For some reason I can never quite recall, we always set up the Christmas tree and nativity scene twelve days before Christmas in our household, but we never put Grandma Penrose's ornaments onto the tree until every member of the family who is coming home for Christmas has arrived."

"The pieces in the nativity display are beautifully made," Charlie said. "The detail is incredible, right down to the expressions on the faces of the donkey and the cow in the byre."

"Aren't they wonderful? The figurines are hand-painted fine porcelain. I have heart palpitations every time the twins go near them. The ornaments for the tree are lovely too."

Across the room, George hung a porcelain dove high on the tree. Jake was next, hanging a drummer boy for himself and an angel for his absent younger brother, Luke.

"My husband's mother had the gift of foresight," Mrs Penrose said. "She gave us the entire set of decorations to celebrate our first Christmas together, telling us there was one for each child we would have. Of course, I thought it was wishful thinking at the time, but we did end up with the same number of children as ornaments, and each ornament hints at the child's character. A dove for George, the peace-maker." Her voice dropped to a whisper. "A drummer-boy for Jake, who has a tendency to drum up mischief, although his heart is true. The angel is for Luke, who was born to do good works."

Grace took up three ornaments and hung them in the middle of the tree, followed by the twins in solemn synchrony.

"I thought Grace's cross meant she would be pious, but it soon became clear that the cross was a medical symbol rather than a religious one. And finally, two sweet cherubs and a pair of shepherds." Mrs Penrose wiped a tear from her eye. "I'm not sure if you know …"

"Cherubs for Rosemary and Lily," Charlie said gently, to save Mrs Penrose from having to explain that her two youngest daughters had died of measles as children. "Why shepherds for the twins?"

Grace answered. "The twins discovered an unexpected passion for farming, after helping their uncle with his orchard and sheep farm last summer. And now, it's time to place the star on top of the tree. Whose turn is it this year, Mama?"

Paul darted over to the box to grab the star. "It's my turn to put the star up this year."

"No, it isn't. It's my turn." Peter jostled his brother for the star. "Paul did it last year when Grace wasn't here."

"I placed the star for Grace last year," Paul reasoned, "so it must be my turn to do it for myself this year."

"Boys, boys, enough squabbling," Mrs Penrose pleaded. "Must we have this argument every year? I have decided that it will be Charlie's turn this year to acknowledge him as part of our family."

Charlie placed the star with due ceremony before rejoining Grace and her mother. "It all looks wonderful. I appreciate being included in your family traditions."

Doctor Penrose took up the book from the sideboard and settled into his armchair. "Gather around, everyone. Time to read from *A Christmas Carol*."

Grace slipped out to the kitchen to retrieve her engagement ring, which she had left on the windowsill while she was washing dishes. The soft bass of her father's voice rose and fell with the familiar words from the drawing room.

The ring was not on the sill. Grace checked behind the set of drawers under the window, which held crockery and cutlery.

From the drawing room, Peter's voice chimed in with one of his favourite lines. "Every idiot who goes about with 'Merry Christmas' on his lips should be boiled with his own pudding, and buried with a stake of holly through his heart." Peter loved the book with a passion and knew it off by heart.

Grace went down on her hands and knees, searching behind cupboards, in cracks in the floor, and under mats. Her precious engagement ring was not there. She searched with growing alarm, opening the window and looking outside, then checking other windowsills in case she had misremembered where she put it.

Her father reached the dramatic scene in which Scrooge's deceased partner visited him, draped in rattling chains, to warn Scrooge of the evil of his ways.

Grace burst into the drawing room. "Has anyone seen my engagement ring?"

Trickery

Charlie reached Grace's side in two long strides. "When did you last have the ring on, Grace?"

"I left it on the windowsill while I was washing dishes." Grace choked back tears. "I've looked everywhere in the kitchen, but it's gone."

Charlie searched a row of surprised and concerned expressions before settling on one with a hint of mischief. "Do you know where Grace's engagement ring is, Jake?"

Grace spun to face her tormentor. "Jake Penrose, if you have taken my ring I will force-feed you brussels sprouts until you beg for mercy."

Jake crossed one leg over the other with slow deliberation. "Calm down, Grace. I thought it might liven up Christmas if we set your fiancé a little festive mystery to solve to prove his worth. If Charlie can find the ring by the end of our family feast on Christmas Eve, I will bow before you and acknowledge his superior skills as a detective."

"That's not fair, Jake," Doctor Penrose said. "You haven't given Charlie any clues, and he has an entire house to search, with Christmas Eve only two days away."

"I'll give him a clue if you wish. Think of things that Grace likes about Christmas. So, Charlie, do you accept the challenge, or do you admit your detecting skills are not up to the task?"

"Jake Penrose, I despair of you," Mrs Penrose said. "If Charlie is to be goaded into this impossible game of yours, he ought to have a reward if he succeeds."

The rest of the family agreed, except Jake. "If Charlie finds the ring, he gets to marry Grace," Jake argued. "Isn't that prize enough?"

"Charlie and Grace will be married next month regardless of your trickery," his mother retorted. "You will put up a worthy prize or give the ring back immediately. Otherwise, you will be out on the street on Christmas day with the orphans from Durham House."

"If you insist." Jake thought for a moment. "If Charlie finds the ring, I will give Grace the music box Grandma gave me."

"But you don't like that music box," Grace protested.

"Only because a music box is for girls. I don't know why Grandma thought I would want it. She ought to have given it to you."

"Perhaps she was trying to civilise you," Grace said. "Nevertheless, because I like the music box, I agree to your terms. If Charlie finds the ring, we get the music box and you go down on your knees and beg for our forgiveness. If he fails to find it, we will admit defeat in your pointless little mystery and live happily ever after anyway."

"Not so fast, Grace," Jake said. "If Charlie fails to find the ring, I have to get a proper prize too. I want the pocket watch that Grandpa Penrose gave you."

Grace's fists flew to her hips. "Absolutely not. Grandpa gave me that watch because he wanted me to become a doctor, like him. Why should I give you anything for playing a trick on me by stealing my ring? You ought to be punished, not rewarded."

Jake smirked. "Aha, it seems my sister does not trust her future husband's ability as a detective, after all."

"That's enough, Jake," Charlie said. "Grace loves that watch. Why don't you give her ring back so we can all enjoy Christmas."

The smirk widened. "I didn't think you would concede defeat quite so quickly, Charlie, but I accept your surrender."

"Oh no you don't," Grace snapped. "I trust Charlie's ability to solve any mystery, however ridiculous. We accept the wager."

Charlie hoped Grace wouldn't regret her words, although he was grateful for her confidence in his abilities. The sensible strategy would have been to laugh and refuse to play the game, but that didn't allow for the accumulated years of sibling rivalry.

"It appears that I have a search to conduct." Charlie attempted to give the impression of a man who might as well do as asked, given he had a few minutes to spare.

"We'll help," the twins chorused. "We know every nook and cranny of this house," Paul said. "And everything Grace likes about Christmas too," Peter added. "The Christmas tree," they both said.

The twins bounded across the drawing room to the Christmas tree, shaking the branches and poking through the tinsel. It was only Charlie's quick reflexes that stopped the tree from toppling again as Paul became entangled and fell backwards.

"Be careful, boys," Doctor Penrose said, with a sigh born of long suffering. "We don't want to break anything, including your skulls. Although, after your behaviour today, I care more about you breaking your grandmother's precious ornaments."

After the twins inspected every inch of the tree and shook every ornament, they turned their attention to the nativity scene. They upended Mary and Joseph, poked under baby Jesus in the manger, shook the ox and the donkey, and came close to breaking off an angel's wing, but the ring remained hidden.

Charlie had dropped into an armchair, as if he had all the time in the world, but he kept his eyes on Jake, watching for give-away glances or signs of tension when one of the searchers came close.

Peter tried the bookcase next, sure that the ring would be hidden amongst Grace's favourite Christmas stories. Paul examined the box that had held the ornaments, then disappeared into the hall to inspect the wreath hanging on the front door. Mrs Penrose wandered the room, as if stretching her legs, but it was obvious she was peeking behind every Christmas card and under the twists of tinsel. Doctor Penrose was not so subtle, as he fossicked through a bowl of wrapped chocolates.

"If you ask me," George said, "the boys are barking up the wrong tree. Everyone knows Grace's favourite Christmas activity is gobbling down the thirteen desserts at the Christmas Eve feast."

Charlie thought he had misheard. "*Thirteen* desserts? I can see I am marrying into the right family. I've never had more than one pudding at Christmas in my life. The standard boiled fruit pudding flamed with brandy."

"Another one of Grandma Penrose's marvellous French traditions," George explained. "We always have thirteen desserts for our family feast on Christmas Eve. I expect that is why Jake gave you until the end of the feast to solve the puzzle. He'll slip the ring into one of the desserts, you mark my words. The yule log probably, as Grace loves it above all else."

"Or the profiteroles," Mrs Penrose suggested. "Grace simply cannot resist them."

"The crème brûlée is my pick," Doctor Penrose said. "Jake likes to be the one who flames the top."

Jake watched on with a smug grin, not giving anything away. "Did I not tell you that the Great Christmas Ring Mystery would be fun?"

Grace crossed her arms over her chest. "Honestly, you give the impression that I am a glutton. I only have a little of each dessert, Charlie, as that is the tradition. If you try every dessert, it brings good luck. In this family, you need it."

"Better and better," Charlie said, "but I hope the ring is not damaged by being soaked in cream or flamed in brandy."

"Jake will be buying you a new ring if he doesn't give it back in perfect condition." Mrs Penrose watched Jake's face closely. "I hope you haven't hidden the ring in one of the presents. It wouldn't be fair to hide it in something that won't be opened until Christmas Day."

"It's not in any of the presents." Jake yawned. "You'll never find it, not in a lifetime of searching. Now, dearest family, if you will excuse me, I'm going to my bed to dream of getting my hands on grandfather's watch at long last. Goodnight everyone."

Mrs Penrose shooed the twins to their beds as well. George wished them luck and left for his own home. Charlie saw him to the door and asked if George would stop by his Aunt Sophie's place on the way home, to let her know Charlie was staying here. When Charlie returned to the drawing room, Grace was alone on the sofa, with her eyes closed, humming softly to herself.

Grace opened her eyes as he tiptoed into the room. "I'm sorry I allowed Jake to taunt me into this silly game, Charlie."

"I'll get your ring back, I promise." Charlie sat down close enough to Grace to feel the warmth of her skin through the layers of clothing.

Grace rested her head against his chest and yawned. "It's impossible. Jake could have hidden my ring anywhere. If he hid it in the attic, it could be centuries before somebody finds it again."

"Not quite anywhere," Charlie said. "Jake only had a relatively short time alone, while your parents, George and I were in the dining room, and you and the twins were washing dishes. Twenty minutes at most. The stairs go up over the dining room, which means I would have heard him if he went upstairs. I doubt he risked hiding it outside. Therefore, the ring can only be in the one of the other rooms downstairs. Your father's office and the closets are unlikely, as they have little to do with his clue about Christmas. Therefore, the drawing room is by far the most likely place. I will make a thorough search tomorrow, if I have time."

Grace nestled into his arms. "When you put it logically, it doesn't sound so impossible. I wouldn't discount the closet though, as Jake went in there to get the box of Grandma's ornaments. It would take days to search through everything in the closet, which might have been why Jake was so sure you would never find my ring. And you're forgetting that he might not have hidden the ring yet. That's exactly the kind of trickery he'd stoop to in order to win."

47

Charlie hoped Grace was wrong, because he really did not want to fail her. He rested his head against hers. "What was that tune you were humming, Grace? I don't think I have heard it before."

"It's a Christmas carol that Grandma Penrose used to sing to me in French when I was little. I suppose I was thinking about her and it came to mind. Grandma died when I was still a child and I regret not having learned the words. There are many stories I've forgotten or never thought to ask, and now it is too late. I do miss her and Grandpa. I wish they could have met you."

"Your grandmother would be happy to be remembered so fondly," Charlie said, fighting off a yawn.

"Time for bed. We have a busy day tomorrow, stopping the sale of Durham House, finding my ring, and teaching my brother the virtue of being charitable at Christmas, whether he likes it or not."

Charlie glanced up at the portrait of Grace's grandparents, who smiled down on them from above the mantlepiece. The artist had caught the mischievous gleam in her grandmother's eyes and the determined set to her jaw. The exact expression he saw on his fiancée when he turned to kiss her goodnight.

Ghoulish Revenge

Charlie lay awake in bed, humming the tune of the French carol and vowing to learn the words for Grace's sake. In fact, if he got the words written down and framed, it would make the perfect gift, knowing how much Grandma Penrose meant to Grace. He sank into a deep sleep, having solved one mystery – what he would get Grace for Christmas.

He woke again with a pounding heart, convinced he had heard chains rattling, even though it must have been no more than a dream. The dream was still so fresh that it felt real, even now he was awake. The hazy ghost of Scrooge's partner had appeared, hovering over his bed, rattling chains. When he reached out to it, the ghost had become Mrs Penrose chained to a fence, and lastly – most vividly of all – Grace's grandmother stood beside him, singing the same song he had been humming as he fell asleep.

Darn it if he couldn't still hear the soft rustle of chains. Charlie turned over and shut his eyes. A soft step squeaked on the floorboards outside his room, followed by another squeak further along. Definitely not a dream.

Charlie eased himself from under the bedclothes and tiptoed to the door. He opened the door slowly, wary of creaking hinges. A ghostly figure, all in white, drifted down the hall away from him. He was not a man who believed in ghosts, but the inhuman shape and faint rattle of chains sent a shiver down his spine.

His heart missed a beat as the moon came out from behind a cloud and caught the figure in a soft beam of light through the window at the end of the hall, right outside Jake's room. The moonlight picked out the shapely figure of a woman clad in a long white nightdress and a flowing veil.

Charlie stifled a laugh. The ghost was not dear departed Grandma Penrose, returned from the grave to haunt her grandson, but Jake's sister, bent on revenge. The ethereal figure sparked a memory of the last time Charlie had seen Grace up to mischief wearing only a nightdress – in a lunatic asylum. He had every hope the next time would be far more pleasant, with their wedding night only a month away.

The erstwhile ghost entered Jake's room. Charlie crept to Jake's door, in time to hear Grace shaking the chain gently at the head of her brother's bed, loud enough for his sleeping brain to register, but not enough to startle him from sleep.

Grace let out a low moan before speaking softly in a deep monotone. "Jake Penrose. Repent your sins. Think of the orphans sleeping on the street. Think of your sister lamenting her lost ring. Repent your sins, Jake Penrose." She paused to inspect her brother, who was now tossing and muttering in his sleep. She rattled the chains and repeated her chant a little louder.

Jake cried out and thrashed so violently that he slipped from his bed and fell to the floor. Fortunately, the sheets tangled around his head, obscuring his vision.

Grace fled. She let out a gasp as she hurtled into Charlie, who was standing out of sight beside the door. He clamped his hand over her mouth to stop her screaming, but her eyes merely crinkled at the sight of him as she pushed past and darted into the safety of his bedroom. Charlie was almost back at his own doorway when Jake stumbled out of his room. Charlie whirled around, so it would look as if he had come to his door at the sound of the commotion.

"Who's there?" Jake said, his voice quavering. "Charlie?"

"I thought I heard a thump," Charlie said. "Are you all right, Jake? You look as if you've seen a ghost." He heard muffled snorts of laughter behind him and coughed to cover the sound.

"Someone was in my room. Was it you?"

"I wasn't in your room, I swear," Charlie answered honestly. "You must have had a nightmare. Charles Dickens' Christmas story can have that effect, I find. Good night, Jake. Pleasant dreams."

Jake stood in the hall, uncertain. "Er, yes, good night."

Charlie closed his door. Warm arms slipped around his waist. He lifted the veil from the ghost's face and kissed deliciously un-ghostly lips. "Go to bed, my wicked little Ghost of Christmas Present, or your parents will have me thrown out of the house."

"Four weeks, one day and twelve hours to go, Detective Pyke, then you will be all mine," Grace whispered, before she slipped from his clutches. At the door, she cast a cautious glance up the hall, then vanished in a trail of white.

Charlie breathed in the lingering scent of rosewater. He slipped back into bed, knowing he would not sleep anytime soon.

When Charlie woke again, soft dawn light filtered through the curtains. He washed and dressed quickly, then crept down the stairs, not knowing what time the Penrose family rose on the day before Christmas Eve.

Jake was at the table, drinking coffee and looking like he'd been dragged backwards through a patch of gorse.

"Rough night, Jake?"

Jake waved a hand at the coffee pot. "Morning, Charlie. I had an extraordinarily vivid nightmare last night, which woke me and kept me awake. How did you sleep?"

"I am happy to say I had nothing but the most delightful of dreams. I must have a clear conscience." Charlie poured coffee and kept a straight face.

"I wish I could say the same." Jake yawned, then took another long slurp of coffee. "I see now that I have behaved badly. Not only over

51

Grace's ring, but in not being more concerned about the orphans' home. I have decided to tackle Spragg on the matter and not relent until Spragg agrees to an extension of the eviction deadline. I would rather be dismissed from my position than work for a man who would evict orphans onto the street at Christmas."

"Good for you, Jake. You will sleep easier, I'm sure." Charlie couldn't wait to tell Grace that her ghost had worked its magic.

"Look, Charlie, about the ring. I'll give it back. I hid it as a bit of fun, not realising Grace would be so upset."

Charlie sipped his coffee and weighed up the risks. "No need, Jake. I plan to find the ring, because Grace rather fancies the music box and I have my honour to defend. But if you truly want to make amends, tell me how we can stop the sale of Durham House."

Jake hesitated. "Mr Spragg cannot stop the sale, if that is what you hope, once the buyer and seller have reached an agreement. Don't look at me that way, Charlie. I cannot disclose the parties to the sale, especially not if Grace plans to harass them."

Charlie knew better than to push the matter, but he was resolved to get hold of the purchaser's copy of the contract somehow, even if he had to remove it from Spragg's office while Jake was distracted. If nothing else, they could rip it up to buy a little time, as there would be no time to redraft the contract before Christmas.

Jake rose from the table, setting his cup down with a sigh. "I must get to work. No rest for the wicked. Not like Grace, who seems to be enjoying a long sleep in this morning."

Charlie finished his own coffee and went to see if Grace's Aunt Sophie was up. George had told his aunt last night that Charlie would be paying a visit.

Calling on a lady this early in the morning would be considered uncivilised in most circumstances, but Charlie knew Sophie from when he had lived in Wellington. They had spent long hours in each other's company, alongside other volunteers, distributing leaflets for the women's suffrage cause. Charlie had acted as security at many a heated suffrage meeting, putting him in her good books. In return, Sophie had shown him great kindness, in asking him for meals to supplement the meagre offerings of Charlie's landlady and encouraging him to pursue Grace Penrose even when the distance between them seemed impossible.

Sophie (as she had insisted he call her, though she was twice Charlie's age) was standing at the kitchen window, waving him in. She settled him at the kitchen table with a cup of tea and a plate of freshly scrambled eggs, oozing ham and cheese. He was grateful for the food, since last night's roast lamb was a distant memory.

"Delicious," Charlie said, tucking in. "My apologies for the late change of plan last night and for my rudeness in turning up early and interrupting your breakfast."

"Think nothing of it, Charlie," Sophie said. "Now that all my children have left home, I have only myself and my husband to look after. George told me about Durham House being sold. Is that why you wanted to see me?"

"No, although it is the reason I had to come early, as we have a busy day ahead. I wanted to ask you if you knew the words to a French carol, which Grace's grandmother used to sing to her." Charlie had hummed no more than a bar or two before Sophie joined in, singing in French.

"My mother's favourite carol," Sophie said. "It's one of the earliest carols written, I believe. I haven't heard it since my mother passed away. I'm surprised Grace recalls it, as I am the only one of Elisabeth Penrose's children who showed an interest in her French origins. The others, including Grace's father, pretended the family was British to the core. Honestly, you'd think the Battle of Waterloo was yesterday, not three-quarters of a century ago."

"Grace only remembers the tune," Charlie said. "That's why I am here. I thought it would make a nice present for her if I had the words to the carol written down and framed. She misses her grandmother."

"How thoughtful of you." Sophie pushed her breakfast plate aside and went to find a sheet of paper. "Do you want the words in French or English?"

"Better make it English." Charlie scooped up the last of the egg while reading her words upside down from across the table. "Ox, donkey, angels, Mary … oh, I see, it's about the birth of Jesus in the stable."

Sophie tapped the pencil on her chin, recalling the last lines of the carol. "There, all done. Grace will be pleased. She and her grandmother adored each other."

They exchanged news for a short time, then Charlie thanked Sophie and went back to the Penrose's house.

Grace and her mother passed him on their way out to go shopping, giving Charlie the opportunity to have a quiet word with her twin brothers. He found them rummaging through the closet in search of Grace's missing ring, leaving a jumble of items piled up behind them in the hallway.

Having seen Peter's beautiful calligraphy, Charlie engaged his services to copy the words of the French carol onto a stiff sheet of quality paper. Paul, with his exceptional drawing skills inherited from his grandfather, was hired to create an illustrated border.

Charlie made the twins promise to tidy the closet and not resume the search for the ring until he returned. Thus, not only would Charlie have his present for Grace, but the twins would have a little spending money, and Mrs Penrose would have a peaceful day when she returned from shopping. A job well done.

With a few minutes to spare before his next task for the day, Charlie visited the drawing room again to conduct his own search while nobody else was there.

Acquisitions

Grace had no regrets about her ghostly antics the previous night. Besides being fun, she hoped the fright might prick her brother's conscience, which would do him the world of good.

She snuck down the stairs, avoiding the squeaky boards, and put her ear to the open door to eavesdrop on Jake and Charlie at the breakfast table. To her delight, the chain-rattling trick had worked. Jake's "nightmare" had provoked him to action on the sale of Durham House.

Grace's mood was further improved by overhearing Charlie reaffirm his desire to find the precious engagement ring. He sounded sure he could do it, despite Jake's equally firm belief that Charlie had no chance of finding the ring. Grace hoped Charlie was right, as Jake would be unbearably smug if he won. She left them to their talk and sneaked back upstairs to prepare for the day ahead.

After a long and luxurious bath, Grace chose a pretty gown of white cotton and lace, embroidered with roses. The gown had been a gift from her ever-hopeful mother, but Grace rarely wore it, because she had an allergy to ruffles and puffed sleeves. The gown was a far cry from her usual practical choice of a fitted white shirtwaist and plain grey skirt, but it was the perfect outfit for high-class shopping and extracting information from gentlemen. She even allowed the maid to pile her hair up into the latest style, before pinning her daintiest summer hat on top. When the artistry was complete, Grace hardly recognised herself in the mirror.

Her mother was waiting downstairs. Her jaw dropped at the sight of her daughter's feminine flounces, but she restrained her reaction to a simple comment on how beautiful Grace looked. Mrs Penrose stepped around the mess the twins were making in the hallway as if it wasn't there, averting her eyes and not letting her saintly smile falter.

Charlie passed them on his way into the house. His eyes boggled at her gown, but he made no comment. Grace had the distinct sense that her fiancé was up to something, but she let it pass. Charlie was always up to something, and it usually turned out for the best.

Grace linked arms with her mother and set forth on their expedition to the wedding department of the most illustrious shopping emporium in Wellington, Kirkcaldie & Stains. Grace planned to make short work of the shopping by the simple expedient of saying yes to whatever her mother suggested. She could not imagine why she hadn't thought of this simple strategy before. Ordinarily, Grace loathed shopping, but with this new approach, efficiency was guaranteed.

The bells of St Paul's chimed as Grace and her mother reached the end of Molesworth Street, opposite Parliament Buildings. They crossed the intersection between a slow-moving dray and a fast-moving messenger boy on a bicycle.

"You're very quiet this morning, Grace," Mrs Penrose said. "I hope you haven't had a falling out with Charlie."

"Not at all, Mama. I am worried about the sale of Durham House. I cannot believe Jake cares so little for the orphans' welfare."

"You underestimate your brother, Grace. Jake is in a difficult position, caught between a demanding employer and his own conscience. I have talked to him at length about the way young Mr Spragg is conducting business. I would rather see him out of work for a time than continue in a position that brings him nothing but regret. Jake says he cannot afford to risk his reputation by leaving without adequate reason or a good reference."

"Surely this latest sale is reason enough?" Grace squeezed her mother's arm. "Do you really plan to chain yourself to the fence outside the orphans' home if the sale goes ahead?"

"Do you doubt me? I've faced up to men in power before, as you know. The women's suffrage cause will not be won by signatures on a petition alone."

Grace kissed her mother's cheek. She may be small, but she was feisty, and Grace was inordinately proud of her. "I'm so fortunate to have you as my mother, but I do hope the matter can be resolved without anyone being chained to a fence, especially not on Christmas Eve."

"I have other options in mind before it comes to that," Mrs Penrose said. "I have an idea who the buyer might be. After we have finished shopping, I intend to pay him a visit."

"Mother, dearest, I hope you were not planning to go without me? And why not immediately, as the matter is urgent?"

"If you insist," her mother replied, with another saintly smile. "Holliman Construction has offices near the wharves. I know from your brother that young Mr Spragg has had dealings with Holliman before. I have told Jake I do not approve. Theodore Holliman has a reputation for buying grand old buildings on large plots of land, only to demolish the buildings in order to replace them with long rows of terraced houses or commercial premises. I suppose it is a more efficient use of land for our growing population, but I fear we'll end up with slums worse than London if he is allowed to continue."

"How do you know so much about Holliman's business activities?"

"I have my sources. I hadn't heard of the man until a couple of years ago, but since then he has purchased at least half a dozen properties, to my knowledge. An acquaintance of mine sold him their lovely home after her husband died. The poor man was on his deathbed when Spragg came knocking on her door, wanting to buy the house on Holliman's behalf. He didn't even wait until her husband was cold in the ground."

Grace could scarcely believe that a man could stoop so low, but her mother was not one to exaggerate. No wonder her mother thought Jake should not work for Spragg.

"I'm not saying I condone Spragg's behaviour," Mrs Penrose continued, "but I do not know all the circumstances. It may be that he knew the family personally and realised the lady in question would be eager to sell. She was willing to accept a low price, because she had no family in New Zealand and was desperate to return to her own family in England after her husband's untimely death."

"I doubt Spragg approached her out of friendship alone," Grace countered. "Spragg and Holliman must make a fortune from their property dealings. How will you find out if Holliman is buying Durham House?"

"Leave it to me, Grace. You are not the only woman in this family with a few tricks up her sleeve."

Quarter of an hour later, they were seated in front of the desk of Mr Theodore Holliman himself. Mrs Penrose had announced herself as the Secretary of the Society for the Preservation of Heritage Buildings and requested a meeting, in a tone of voice that brooked no refusal.

"You're even more brazen than me," Grace whispered, as they waited. "Well done, Mama. I am in awe."

"I am not the least bit brazen, Grace," her mother whispered back. "I am the secretary of that society. I hope you didn't think I would lie to achieve my goal?"

A rotund gentleman in a scarlet waistcoat entered the room. Under a prominent nose, his handlebar moustache was waxed and pinched into such a sharp point that it risked skewering an unwary wife to death.

"Mrs Penrose and Miss Penrose," Mr Holliman boomed, with unexpected bonhomie. "How charming of you to honour me with a visit. You'll be wanting a donation to your fine society, I don't doubt. My clerk will attend to it when you depart. Naturally, I am delighted to support heritage causes, young though our fine city may be. I told

58

the Mayor so last week, when he dined at my home. My business may entail the removal of ramshackle eyesores about town, but I am no philistine when it comes to architecture of true distinction. I am proud to contribute to the betterment of our fair city."

When Holliman paused to take an overdue breath, Mrs Penrose pounced. "Quite so, Mr Holliman. I heard a rumour you intend to purchase Durham House. Is that correct?"

Mr Holliman took a seat and reappraised his audience. "You are exceptionally well informed, Mrs Penrose, as the sale is not yet general knowledge. In fact, I have not yet received the signed documents, although I understand the owner has agreed to my offer. An unfortunate case of dry rot in the support beams, according to the survey report commissioned by the owner's agent. He practically begged me to make him an offer, and it suited me to oblige. Fortunately, it is not a building of any architectural or historical merit, as I am sure you will agree. I assure you I will create a new structure the city will be proud of."

"Dry rot. Oh dear." Mrs Penrose let out a long sigh. "I suppose the building is not worth much in that case. I wonder if you would consider passing on the sale, as the Society has been looking for new premises. The central location of Durham House would suit us very well."

Holliman allowed a few seconds to tick by as he pretended to consider her request. "I am afraid that would not be possible, Mrs Penrose. As a man of honour, I could not withdraw from the sale once it is agreed. As it happens, I am already committed to the future development of the site. I am sure I could find you another location far more suitable for your needs."

"How kind of you, Mr Holliman," Mrs Penrose replied. "However, there is no need to put you to any trouble on our behalf. It was nothing but a momentary whim on my part when I heard that Durham House might be available. I thank you for your time and generosity."

Mr Holliman smiled at them, his eyes twinkling as if their company had been the highlight of his morning. He held the door open and wished them a good day. Grace was aware of Holliman's eyes on their backs as they walked down the corridor, stopping at the clerk's desk to collect the promised donation, which was generous indeed.

Grace had been fully prepared to loathe the man, but he was much more charming than she had expected. Holliman clearly believed his business benefitted the city. If he truly was buying buildings with structural defects for a fair price, there was little they could do to stop him. Even paying below the odds to her mother's friend might be no more than sharp business practice, as the bereaved widow had been eager to sell quickly and return to her family in England.

When they were across the road and out of sight, Grace embraced her mother. "You were magnificent, Mama."

"Thank you dear, but our visit achieved little. Aside from the donation, the only thing gained was the knowledge that the buyer of Durham House would not be swayed by the plight of adorable orphans."

Grace took up her mother's arm. "You discovered several useful facts, including the name and views of the buyer. As Charlie always says, an investigation proceeds by narrowing the possibilities until the solution becomes clear. In this case, it seems the building owner was the one who was keen to sell because of the state of the building. Spragg, as the owner's agent, commissioned the valuation and property inspection. Now, no more talk of rotting buildings. Let's go shopping for my wedding."

Mother and daughter soon arrived at the broad Italianate frontage of Kirkcaldie & Stains on Lambton Quay.

Grace would normally prefer to conduct an autopsy on a decaying body than go shopping. However, her wedding was a special occasion and her mother had excellent taste. Grace soon found herself agreeing to her mother's suggestions with genuine delight. She lost herself to the extent of shedding tears of joy over the silkiness of the fabric and the beauty of the lace that her mother picked out for Grace's wedding gown. By the time they were selecting ribbons for the bouquets and card for the place settings, Grace was – to her surprise – thoroughly enjoying herself.

"Are you quite well, Grace?" her mother asked, as Grace fingered the thick, creamy card stock and imagined her name on it beside Charlie's.

"Never happier, my dear Mama. You have been a saint to put with me all these years. Any other mother would have disowned me for my unladylike interests. Yet, here you are, organising my wedding with the same serenity and kindness you have shown me all my life. I don't deserve you, but I do love you."

Mrs Penrose flushed a becoming pink. She removed her glove and put a hand on Grace's forehead. "No fever. I can only put it down to the good influence of Charlie Pyke. I am delighted you two found each other, even if I quail at accounts of your exploits together."

Fortunately, her mother didn't know a tenth of what she and Charlie got up to in their investigations in Dunedin, unless one or the other ended up in hospital. Ignorance is bliss when it comes to minimising parental heart palpitations.

Grace couldn't help herself. She hugged her mother in front of the gathered shop assistants and felt a fierce joy as her mother hugged her back. Her mother suppressed a chuckle and adjusted her hat.

She took the cream card from Grace and passed it back across the counter to the manager of Kirkcaldie & Stains. "We'll take this one. That will be all for today, thank you."

As their purchases had piled up, the initial shop assistant had given way to the department supervisor. As the till continued to ring merrily, word had passed to the store manager, who had come to officiate over proceedings. He was now rubbing his hands with glee, albeit in the subdued and entirely decorous manner of the manager of the premier establishment in the city, if not the country. A liveried boy stood to attention behind him, balancing a stack of bags and boxes and rolls of fabric. Beaming shop attendants fanned out on either side, flushed from fetching and carrying.

"It has been our pleasure to serve you, Mrs Penrose," the store manager said, with a modest bow. "I shall ensure that your purchases are wrapped and delivered this afternoon."

Their mission complete, Grace and her mother thanked the staff and swept down the stairs. Grace felt almost as euphoric as the day Charlie had proposed, if only because the dream-like concept of a wedding was now as real as the feel of the soft satin between her fingers.

The doorman tipped his top hat as he held the door open for them. Mrs Penrose exited the shop, looking momentarily dizzy from the unexpected success of the expedition. She drew Grace away from the bustle of passers-by on Lambton Quay. "Dearest Grace, I haven't enjoyed myself this much in a long time. I cannot wait to watch you walk down the aisle on your father's arm. I am proud of you and all you have achieved, my dear. I hope you know that."

"Even after all the trouble I have caused?" Grace ventured.

"You have given us endless amusement, which has been more than enough to offset the occasional moments of embarrassment and the rare instances of abject terror. Do you remember when you fell out of the tree onto Mrs Willard's picnic?"

"I have never been very happy at heights since," Grace admitted.

"I thought I would burst from holding the laughter in, once your father had checked that all your limbs were intact."

This was news to Grace, who had thought her mother was mortified by her untimely fall from the tree. "How could I forget landing on Mrs Willard's prize-winning Victoria sponge and splattering the vicar with cream? I was so embarrassed, I walked the long way to school for years to avoid the Willard house."

"Did you? How amusing. Mrs Willard always thought it was Jake on account of her shortsightedness and the fact that you were wearing a pair of Jake's old trousers. Jake was blamed for rather a lot of your adventures, as I recall."

"I wish I had known that. Poor Jake." Grace had never thought of it from Jake's point of view before. She considered any trouble she got him into was fair retribution for the torments he put her through. "We both thought you must love George the best, because he was never in any trouble and we were never out of it."

"Oh, Grace, what a silly thing for you to believe. Your father and I loved you all equally. George was so well behaved compared to the rest of you, we wondered if there might be something wrong with him, but he turned out fine, as did all of you. You'll only understand when you have your own children." Her mother kissed her cheek. "I've had a lovely time this morning, my dear, but I won't ask you to take tea with me, as you have other matters on your mind. I hope you and Charlie can stop the sale of Durham House."

"We will do our best." Grace waited until her mother disappeared into the crowd. We have one last chance, she thought, and failure was not an option.

The city clocks chimed eleven times. Grace had to find Charlie without delay.

Inquisitive Orphans

When Charlie left the house after dropping off the French carol to the twins, he was humming the carol and feeling joyous. The day was sunny, with a feather-light breeze to keep the heat at bay. He paused to sniff the roses, which twisted their way around the veranda posts, and imagined the sweet satisfaction of slipping the engagement ring back on Grace's finger.

But he was getting ahead of himself, with a busy day ahead.

First, he had promised to accompany Tom and Eva to Durham House, because they were nervous about meeting so many unfamiliar children. Charlie glanced at his pocket watch. He was cutting it fine to reach the Crockett's house in time.

Charlie ran down the front steps and pushed through the gate in the picket fence. Fortunately, the Crockett's home was close by. Five minutes later, he was looking down on a row of a single-storey wooden boxes, tucked into a shallow gully under the shadows of Tinakori Hill. The morning sun had not yet reached the windows and the sun would likely disappear again by afternoon. Water from recent rain sat in pools on the packed earth. If it was like this in summer, he could only imagine how damp and cold it must be in winter.

How very different these simple cottages were from the nearby houses on Tinakori Road. Most of the local houses were like the Penrose's home, which was an elegant two storey wooden structure, with bay windows on the lower level, arched windows above, and a veranda looking out over a flourishing garden.

Charlie recalled his first sight of the Penrose's house, which had hammered home the stark contrasts between Grace and himself. Grace was the daughter of a prominent doctor, whereas Charlie's father was a small-town policeman and his mother had spent her life being slighted for being half-Chinese. Charlie's childhood home was a squat stone cottage, looking out onto the dry, rocky hills of Central Otago. He had always hoped Grace would visit one day, knowing she would love the wildness of the rocky landscape and the huge skies above. He had never expected that he might take Grace there himself, as his wife.

As Charlie walked down the track past the row of cottages, he spotted a middle-aged woman, bent beyond her years, washing plates at the outside tap. The water drained away into an open ditch. "Good morning. Would you be Mrs Crockett?"

She nodded and waved him over. "Good morning. You'll be Mr Pyke, and most welcome here, after helping our Martha with the wee ones on the steamer from Christchurch. We're in a fluster this morning, what with Mr Crockett all of a haste to leave early this morning and quite forgetting his notecase and the buttie I made for him. Our Martha had to take them down to the city. My husband's head's in a spin over this property sale and no mistake. There now, don't you mind me prattling on. Go on in, Mr Pyke."

Martha was still flushed from her dash to her father's workplace. She plaited Eva's hair with quick fingers at the tiny kitchen table. "Good morning, Mr Pyke."

"Do call me Charlie." Charlie sat beside Tom by the fireplace. "How do you like your new home, Tom?"

"Aunt Martha says it's not the size of the house that matters, but the size of the hearts inside it."

An impressively diplomatic answer from a boy who was six years (and ten months) old. Charlie noticed Tom's small valise standing beside a straw pallet mattress, which was pushed upright against the far wall. These worker's cottages only had two bedrooms. Mr Crockett and his wife would have one, while Martha and now Eva would share the other, probably sharing a bed.

Charlie hated to see little Tom down in the dumps. "Miss Penrose grew up near here with five brothers. She told me the children had great fun playing hide and seek on Tinakori Hill and in the Botanical Gardens. On a rainy day, you can walk to the Colonial Museum, which is quite marvellous."

Tom kicked his good leg against the wooden bench. "I suppose so. It was very flat where we lived before." He kicked for a few more seconds, choosing his words carefully. "Aunt Martha says a man can feel like a king if he is content with what he has, but a king might feel like a pauper if he is always dissatisfied."

"Your Aunt Martha is a very clever lady."

"She must have been thinking of Mr Spragg," Tom said. "He lives like a king, but Aunt Martha told Grandma he is the most miserable old wretch who ever lived."

Charlie rubbed his hand over his mouth to conceal a grin. "How do you know Mr Spragg lives like a king, Tom?" Spragg's office had certainly showed no sign of wealth, or even common comforts.

"Me and Eva went to have a look last night before bedtime. Mr Spragg lives near here in a huge house all to himself. Two storeys and more windows than I can count." Tom lowered his voice still further, so Charlie had to lean close to hear. "We were being detectives, like you. Eva let me sit on her shoulders so I could see in a window. Mr Spragg has shiny candlesticks on a long table and a whole scuttle of coal by the fireplace and a big cupboard with a glass front and dozens of glasses and fancy bottles. The room next to it had paintings on the wall and thick curtains and two clocks and rugs. Mr Spragg must not even use the room, as the armchairs were covered."

So much for the impression Charlie had that Spragg's business was struggling to make ends meet. The man must be making money, and plenty of it, unless he had inherited wealth. More likely, Spragg was simply too much of a miser to share his profits with his hard-working employees.

Martha paused mid-plait. "I heard that, Tom Crockett. So that's where you two disappeared to after your supper last night. You had me worried, with dark coming on. It is rude to look into other people's houses, Tom. Indeed, it is against the law. I'm sure real detectives never break the law when they are investigating."

"Your Aunt Martha is right," Charlie said sternly, ignoring all the times he had skirted the law for the sake of justice. "Detectives cannot be caught breaking the law or they might be sent to gaol the same as real criminals."

Charlie would have to have a word with Tom and Eva to discourage these inquisitive young children from getting into trouble on his behalf. He knew it was his own fault, as he had told them detective tales on the steamer voyage to pass the time and cheer them up. With a guilty jolt, he remembered he had been foolish enough to show them his lock picks, during a particularly gruelling part of the journey. Hopefully, they had been too seasick to recall it.

Martha tied off Eva's second plait and gathered her satchel. "Come along, you two rascals, or we'll be late for class. What are your plans for the day, Charlie?"

"I'm going back to Mr Spragg's office to see what I can do about delaying the sale of Durham House, to give you time to find a new home for the orphans."

"In that case, let us delay no more." Martha led the party out of the house. She made Eva and Tom stop outside in the daylight to check that they were spick and span. After rubbing soot off Tom's nose and straightening the ribbon on Eva's bonnet, Martha declared them ready to go.

Charlie thought they made a winsome group, holding their heads proudly despite their darned and patched clothes. If only the owner of Durham House could see them now, he might be made to understand the consequences of his decision to sell.

"We are late." Martha glanced at her nephew's twisted foot uncertainly. "Quick as you can, Tom, but not if it causes you pain."

"It would be faster if Charlie carried me … Mr Pyke, I mean." Tom's eyes sparkled. "Please, Aunt Martha."

"Come on, Master Tom. It's not far." Charlie swung Tom onto his shoulders and strode off beside Martha.

Eva fell into step beside him. "Promise me you won't visit Mr Spragg's house, Mr Pyke. Mr Spragg is not a nice man."

"I won't be calling on him at his home, Eva. Mr Spragg left town yesterday and he will not be back until this afternoon."

Eva shook her head. "He's here. I saw him last night." The girl shuddered and darted a glance around, as if she feared Spragg might spring out upon them. "At least, I think it was a man. It might have been a ghoul."

"I cannot believe you two went to Mr Spragg's house," Martha said. "It was very naughty."

Eva turned pleading eyes on Charlie. "But Mr Spragg is selling the orphans' home. Grandpa says Mr Spragg needs the money from the sale, so me and Tom went to see if he was so very poor that he needed the money more than the orphans did. He doesn't. Mr Spragg is not poor at all, just mean."

"Eva, that's enough," Martha scolded. "We have no right to interfere in his business."

"Eva, you must promise your Aunt Martha never to look into a stranger's house again." Charlie waited for Eva to nod. "Having said that, I would like to hear what you saw, if that is all right with your aunt. It might be important."

Eva glanced at her aunt for approval before sharing her recollections. "It was unholy terrifying, Mr Pyke. The room Tom looked in might have been an ordinary rich man's house, but the room I looked in was scary." Eva glanced sideways, her brows low over her eyes, presumably trying to judge whether Martha was going to scold her for making up tall tales.

"Go on, Eva," Charlie said gently.

"I know it was wrong to spy, but Aunt Martha was in tears last night at losing her job and the orphans' home. I thought if me and Tom could see what Mr Spragg was like, we could make a plan to help her."

"That's kind of you, Eva, but I hope you won't try anything so dangerous again. Miss Penrose and I have a plan to deal with Mr Spragg. It would help us to know exactly what you saw."

"There wasn't much light, and thin curtains covered the window, but I am sure I saw the shapes of three people in the room. They weren't moving, and they were shrouded, like ghosts. Or they might have been mourners, because I'm sure one woman was dead. She was laid out on a bench as you would a corpse, covered with a sheet from head to foot. I'm not making it up, honest. There were several long boxes, like coffins, on the floor. I dare not think what horrors were inside them."

Eva was close to tears now, despite Martha's comforting arm around her thin shoulders.

"I'm not sure what you saw, Eva," Charlie said softly, "but I believe you. I promise you I will find out, if only to ease your mind."

"That was not the worst of it," Eva whispered. "While I was watching, a man came into the room – all thin and hunched and creepy. It must have been Mr Spragg, for Grandpa says he lives alone. When his pale face turned to the window, I thought I would turn to stone."

The simple honesty of Eva's words assured Charlie that she was not a foolish child making up wild stories. Eva truly believed she had seen a man, but perhaps it had been a manservant rather than Spragg. Either way, Charlie would be visiting Mr Spragg as soon as he could, both to set Eva's mind at rest and to uncover the truth about what Spragg was up to.

"Did the man see you, Eva?"

"I don't think so, Mr Pyke. I was up a tree, hidden by the leaves. The face turned away again before I lost my grip and fell. You'd never catch me back there, even if you promised me a handful of silver shillings."

"We're nearly at Durham House now, Eva. Can you promise me you will put aside what you saw at Mr Spragg's house and try to have fun with the children you meet today?" Charlie hoped rather than believed that forgetting would be so easy for the girl.

Martha had guided their little group through a pleasant neighbourhood of streets, churches and schools, before cutting down a steep set of steps to the less salubrious spot where Durham House stood in sight of the railway line. The building was decades old, but it looked sturdy enough.

Charlie swung Tom down from his shoulders. When he saw the lad's face, he wished he hadn't allowed Eva to tell her scary tale. Tom looked up at the imposing door in front of him and stayed close to Charlie, clinging to his trouser leg.

"Will you come in with us, Mr Pyke?" Tom whispered.

"Of course I will, Tom, but only for a while."

Martha took hold of Eva's hand. "Perhaps we could persuade Mr Pyke to spend a few minutes telling my pupils what it is like to be a detective."

"Of course," Charlie said, although he had come prepared with magic tricks, not detective tales. But how could he refuse when Eva and Tom looked so excited? Starting out in a new place was always hard. Tom would have it harder than most, because his deformed foot would mark him out as different and less able to join in fast-paced activities.

Inside Durham House, children milled around and played games, ready to start their school day. On the stage, the choir had gathered to begin rehearsals. Martha explained the choir would be carolling door-to-door on Christmas Eve, spreading musical joy to the residents of Thorndon.

Martha soon had Charlie surrounded by a circle of eager children. He started with the obligatory educational remarks about how important it was to understand science and maths, and above all, how important it was to be able to read and write, in order to become a detective.

The children, naturally, wanted to hear about his most gruesome murder case. At the slight shake of Martha's head, Charlie told them about The Case of the Missing Ship's Parrot. The case had been ridiculously easy to solve, as the thief (a rival captain who coveted the scarlet macaw) had failed to take account of the bird's attachment to its owner and its ability to talk. However, with a judicious amount of embellishment, the tale had the children in giggles. No bloodshed was involved, aside from the parrot bites suffered by the thief.

"Do you have to be big and tough to be a detective?" one of the smaller children asked.

"Not at all," Charlie replied. "You have to be clever and observant. Take your new friends here. Only this morning, Eva and Tom gave me an important clue, which will help me solve a case. Eva was clever enough to realise something was wrong, so they went to investigate. Tom might walk a little slower than other people, but that means he observes things that others don't, which is the mark of a true detective."

The orphans cast admiring glances at Eva and Tom, but Martha's smile seemed rather rigid. Belatedly, Charlie recalled his vow not to encourage risky behaviour. He'd seen a chance to introduce Eva and Tom and seized it without thinking. "The most important part," he continued hastily, "was that Tom and Eva were also clever enough to do no more than observe, because bad people are dangerous. You must always tell a teacher or the police if you see something suspicious." Charlie scoured his mind for a lighter note to finish on. "Mind you, I reckon if Eva had sung a song, the villain would have wept from the beauty of her voice and changed his evil ways on the spot."

"I'd like to hear Eva sing," the littlest orphan said.

Charlie looked at Eva. He had heard Eva singing to soothe a frightened child on the steamer voyage and had been astonished by her lovely voice, but now he worried she would be too shy to sing in front of strangers. He was cursing himself for speaking without thinking again, when Martha saved the day.

"Would you sing if I sang with you, Eva? Shall we sing 'Silent Night'?"

Together Martha and Eva sang, quietly at first and then with more confidence. The children listened, wide-eyed and open-mouthed. The choir stopped their rehearsal and came over.

Charlie realised that Jake Penrose had arrived without him noticing. Jake was at the back of the group of adults, gazing at Martha, as enraptured as the children.

At the end of the carol, everyone clapped, and the choirmaster called, "Brava." A girl from the choir went up to Eva and asked her to join them on stage, while several boys clustered around Tom. Jake backed out towards the door.

Charlie couldn't let Grace's brother leave without hearing what he had come to say. He rose and hurried towards the door. "Jake, wait. What did you want?"

"I came to accuse Martha Crockett of theft, but I've changed my mind."

Sneak Thief

Charlie couldn't believe he had heard Jake correctly. Rather than confront him in front of Martha and the orphans, he took his future brother-in-law out onto the street. "Why would you accuse Martha Crockett of being a thief, Jake? You ought to be praising her for her beautiful voice and sweet character."

When Jake hung his head in response, Charlie took pity on him. "What has been stolen?"

"The sale documents for Durham House. After my nightmare last night, I had second thoughts about the sale. It didn't sit well on my conscience, so I wanted to have another look at the documents. When I went into Mr Spragg's office, I couldn't find the file anywhere, even though I put back it back on his desk myself, as you witnessed. I was the last to leave the office and I am sure I locked up properly. Mr Spragg will be furious. The file contained the purchaser's copy of the deeds. If I cannot find the file, the documents will have to be redrafted and signed again."

"But why do you suspect Martha?" Charlie asked. "You must know Martha would never stoop so low."

"I don't want to think badly of her, but Miss Crockett was the only visitor to the office this morning. She was there early, dropping a notecase to her father, or so she said." Jake grabbed Charlie's arm and started walking towards the central city. "Charlie, you have to help me find the documents. Mr Spragg will dismiss me if I don't find the file by the time he returns this afternoon."

Charlie couldn't resist pointing out the irony of Jake's plea. "You must be desperate if you are asking for help from an inexperienced private detective with uncertain future prospects, especially when I should be committing my time to finding Grace's engagement ring."

"Forget the ring," Jake cried. "I was a fool to have taken it and even more of a fool to have questioned your abilities. If I get down on my knees and beg, will you help me? I will give back Grace's ring, I promise. She's welcome to the music box too."

"Don't worry, Jake, I'll find the documents and the ring." Charlie did not particularly want to return the sale documents to Spragg, but nor did he want to be responsible for Jake losing his position. "Are you sure the file has been stolen? Is it not more likely that Mr Spragg came in early this morning and took the documents?"

Jake shook his head. "Mr Spragg told us he was out of town until this afternoon."

Not according to Eva, Charlie thought. "Do you know if Mr Spragg lives with family?"

"He lives alone. He has no family, as far as I am aware. Certainly, he was the only relative at his father's funeral last year. I'm not sure Mr Spragg has any close friends either, for he told us he spent last Christmas alone. Why do you ask, Charlie?"

"It all helps to paint a picture of a man's character. Tell me about the theft."

"Nothing else is missing," Jake said, "so the thief must have specifically targeted the sale documents for Durham House. I don't want it to be Martha or her father, but it must be somebody connected with orphans' home and Mr Crockett is the only one with access to a key."

Charlie was worried that Jake might be right. He wouldn't blame Mr Crockett or Martha for trying to stop the sale. Anyone associated with Durham House – or indeed any right-thinking citizen – would want to rip the sale documents into shreds. Bad enough to sell such a vital building at any time, but to send out an eviction notice to orphans at Christmas was a blow worthy of Scrooge himself.

74

He said no more until they reached the premises of Marton & Spragg. Charlie urged Jake to let him talk to Mr Crockett, without interruption or accusations.

Mr Crockett answered his questions readily, with no hint of nervousness. "There have been no callers this morning, Mr Pyke. I was out for a time myself, running errands, but I locked the door behind me, as Mr Penrose was out too."

"Your daughter came by, did she not?" Charlie said. "Were you here then?"

"Martha stopped by to deliver a few items I had forgotten this morning. I was on my way out to get the morning newspaper and more ink, so I let her in and told her to shut the door on her way out. I assure you, Mr Pyke, my Martha would never steal anything, not if her life depended on it."

"We know that, Mr Crockett. Your daughter is a credit to you. Might she have left the door open in her hurry to get home?"

"The door was shut when I returned a short time later," Mr Crockett assured him. "Martha is a careful girl. Even if she had left the door open, an intruder would not have been able to access Mr Spragg's office, as that door was locked and I had the key with me."

Charlie examined the doors, but found no evidence that either lock had been picked or forced. Inside Spragg's office, there was none of the usual mess that accompanied a burglary. Everything appeared to be exactly as he had seen it yesterday, except for the missing file. Charlie still thought the most likely explanation was that Mr Spragg had been in early this morning.

Nevertheless, he checked the only other way into the office. To Charlie's surprise, the sash lock on the window was open. When he lifted the lower sash, he saw scrape marks where a slim tool had been forced underneath the bottom of the window to lever it up. A fragment of grey wool had caught on a splinter of wood as the intruder had scrambled into the office.

Charlie put the wool fragment into a twist of paper in order to examine it more closely later. The wool was a dark grey colour, such as commonly used in garments. Both the men from the soup kitchen had worn dark grey trousers, as did Doctor Penrose, and a fair proportion of the male population. Martha wore a grey wool skirt, but then, so did Miss Bentwick, Grace, and the orphan girls. However, Charlie had noticed this morning that Martha's skirt was hanging down at the bottom seam, with a loose strand of wool trailing on the floor.

Charlie turned back to Jake and Mr Crockett, who were watching on with interest. "Well, gentlemen, it is clear you have been burgled. Did you check the sash locks on the windows before you left last night, Jake? This one was open."

"I checked all the other locks, but Mr Spragg is the only one allowed in this office when he is not here. He must have failed to secure the sash lock when he left. I must admit that I am relieved to hear an outsider broke in. It must still be someone from Durham House though. Perhaps those rather intimidating tattooed men from the soup kitchen?"

"Let's not make accusations without proof," Charlie said.

"Who else would want to take the documents and halt the sale? I cannot imagine why the thief took such a risk, when we can simply redraft the documents. All they have gained is a brief delay."

Charlie didn't respond. He was trying to suppress the unwelcome thought of Eva and Tom's little faces peering in the windows of Mr Spragg's house. The children were only trying to help their aunt keep her job at the orphans' home, but their boldness worried him. In truth, Charlie felt guilty for encouraging them with his detective stories. Surely, the children would not have come all the way into the city by themselves to steal the critical documents?

Charlie turned his attention back to the window. He shut the lower sash and turned the handle of the sash lock to the closed position, engaging a small hook behind a locking bar. The lock was a simple mechanism, with a loose fit after years of use. He rattled the window, noting that the shaking had knocked the hook closer to the open position.

"The sash lock isn't very robust," Charlie said. "I suppose it might have been possible to knock the catch open, especially if Mr Spragg hadn't engaged the lock properly when he last closed the window. I need some time to find out who stole the file. Meanwhile, it would be best if you said nothing. I'll try to have an answer for you before your employer returns later this afternoon."

"I am in your debt, Charlie," Jake said. "You will need to be back by three o'clock, when Mr Spragg has told us he plans to return."

"I'll do my best." Charlie's sympathies lay with the thief in this instance. However, he wanted to find the property file, which would give him the crucial information he needed if they were to stop the sale.

After Charlie found the missing property deeds, he would still have to face the difficult decision about what to do with the documents. Give them back to Jake and allow the sale to proceed, or keep them hidden and destroy Jake's career? Whichever way he chose, he was going to risk losing the goodwill of at least one member of the Penrose family. So much for Grace's hopes of a peaceful family Christmas. Still, there was no time to worry about that now. He hoped Grace would be home soon, so they could discuss what was to be done.

After Charlie left the office, he checked the window from the outside. The burglar has been very careful – but not careful enough. In a small patch of grime, he spotted a partial boot mark, which he measured and sketched.

Charlie spent most of the rest of the morning pursuing his investigations. His suspicions regarding the burglar's identity proved correct. When Grace came home at eleven-twenty that morning, Charlie was engrossed in the property file for the sale of Durham House, which he had retrieved from its hiding place.

Grace's face was shining from a brisk walk home, but her delight at seeing him turned to surprise at seeing the file in his hands. "Charlie, how in the name of Zeus did you convince Jake to give you the property file?"

Charlie waved a hand at the spread of teapot, cups, cheese, bread and fruit tarts on the table in front of him. "Jake didn't give the file to me. It was stolen by a burglar, and I stole it back."

Grace poured a cup of tea and topped up his cup. "Jake will have to admit you're a wonderful detective now. I won't ask how and where you found it."

"Best not," Charlie agreed.

"I don't suppose you would consider ripping the deeds into shreds to gain us time?"

Charlie had considered it, but decided that option would be a last resort. He closed the file and changed the subject. "How was your morning of shopping with your mother, Grace?"

"To my astonishment, we had a wonderful time. After interrogating the buyer of Durham House, my mother and I bought a fair proportion of the merchandise in the wedding department of Kirkcaldie & Stains. Wait until you see the gorgeous fabric my mother found for my wedding gown."

Charlie put his teacup down with exaggerated care. "You went to see the man who is buying Durham House? Mr Holliman? You and your mother … alone?"

"Are you not interested in my wedding gown, Charlie?" Grace picked up an apple and rubbed it on a napkin, in an obvious attempt to avoid his gaze.

"Nothing in this world could make me happier than seeing you walking down the aisle on our wedding day, Grace, even if you are dressed in a sugar sack. However, right now, I want to know what the blue blazes you were doing visiting Holliman."

Grace cut the apple into quarters. She crunched into one piece and slid two pieces across the table. Charlie knew her well enough to diagnose a distraction, allowing Grace time to plan her response.

"It was my mother's idea," Grace said.

"Your mother suddenly decided to become a detective?" Charlie did not bother to hide the note of disbelief in his voice.

"She doesn't want the orphans to lose their home any more than we do. Charlie, you should have been there. Mama was magnificent."

Charlie had always thought of Mrs Penrose as a sweet, motherly type, but he was beginning to see that Grace had inherited her strength of character from both sides of the family. If so, there was no point in trying to fight the tide. "You'd better tell me what you two found out."

"My mother talked her way into Holliman's office and asked him straight out if he was buying Durham House, because her society was interested in purchasing it as a meeting place. Apparently, she is the Secretary of the Society for Heritage something-or-other. Holliman admitted he was the buyer, but said she would not want it because Durham House was suffering from dry rot. He made it sound as if he was doing the owner a favour by taking the place off his hands. Mother says Holliman has a record of buying large old houses and demolishing them, allowing him to build a whole row of new buildings on the site. Probably makes a fortune."

"Interesting," Charlie said. "That tallies with the information I've been reading in the property file, which includes a valuation and property inspection report. The report lists a range of building faults, including dry rot, citing the defects as the reason for the low valuation of Durham House. I smell a rat. If Holliman has bribed a property inspector to falsify the report, he may be getting the property at a cheap price."

Charlie's partner in their private detective agency had become an expert in matters of fraudulent business dealings. Over many an evening chat, Charlie had become much more familiar with property values and the many devious ways in which sellers and buyers attempted to dupe each other. A forged or falsified valuation and property inspection was one of the classics.

"Unfortunately, there is a flaw in your theory," Grace said. "Holliman said the owner commissioned the valuation and he was the one who approached Holliman to buy the building. Or rather, the owner's agent did. Perhaps Spragg is the one cheating the owner?"

"Why would he, when he would get a larger commission on a higher sales price? Besides, the owner must be aware of the condition of his own building." Charlie speared a slice of apple with his knife. "Are we so desperate to stop the sale that we are seeing dubious dealings where none exists? The most likely explanation is that the owner and buyer have come to a perfectly legitimate agreement, as is their right."

"Durham House looks to be in reasonable condition to me. I suppose the rot could be in the foundation or framing, such that it's not visible. An inspector might find it, but why wouldn't the matron have mentioned an inspection being done?"

"The leasing agent probably required regular inspections as part of the lease agreement. Do you think Holliman could be convinced to delay the sale, Grace?"

"Definitely not. He held out against my mother, which suggests a strong determination to proceed."

"Tell me about Mr Holliman." Charlie doubted it would do much good, but knowing the potential enemy was always a good start.

"Holliman is hearty and rotund and full of his own importance. His game is finding cheap buildings and making a fortune off them." Grace sliced her second piece of apple into increasingly tiny pieces, seemingly unaware she was taking out her frustration on the fruit. After a pause, she looked down at the pulp and pushed it away. "However, he also genuinely believes he is doing good and making the city a better place by converting dilapidated buildings into new homes and business premises. He was straightforward in his answers, suggesting he had nothing to hide. I did not much care for the man, but nor did I get the impression he was doing anything underhand or illegal, especially if he was telling the truth about the owner commissioning the valuation."

Charlie could understand why Grace was disheartened. Holliman did not sound like the type of man who could be convinced to delay the sale for the sake of a group of orphans. He probably hadn't even inquired about the current tenants of the building he wanted to purchase.

That left them only one other person to appeal to. "Shall we go and talk to the owner of Durham House? His name is Mr Waterstone."

Selling Out

Mr Waterstone's residence was not far away. Their route twisted through the quiet streets of Thorndon until they stood in front of a substantial wooden house on the outskirts of the city. The house was as imposing in size as its neighbours, but had slipped into the first stages of disrepair. Beyond the weeds and overgrown trees, Grace could see patches of peeling paint. She was not yet sure whether this was because of the financial situation of the owner or lack of care, but they were about to find out.

A maid answered the door. At first, she tried to put them off by citing her master's infirmity, but Charlie stood on the doorstep with one foot over the threshold, and showed no signs of being deterred. The maid gave him one last haughty glare before turning to take their calling cards to Mr Waterstone.

The maid returned to take them into the library. "Mr Pyke and Miss Penrose to see you, Mr Waterstone."

The man lying on the chaise longue was grey. Grey with age, grey with pain, grey eyes contemplating them as they entered the room. Mr Waterstone's body was propped upright with the help of several plump pillows and covered with a blanket of grey wool. Aside from his face, all Grace could see were his hands, which were twisted into claws around swollen knuckles, barely able to hold the book he was reading. Even so, his eyes followed their entrance into his private domain with a flare of interest and a sharpness that warned Grace not to underestimate Mr Waterstone. She was not surprised to note that legal tomes lined the library walls.

Mr Waterstone put the book down and nudged the calling cards around on the side table so that he could read them. "Mr Charles Pyke, private detective. Miss Grace Penrose, medical student. I am at a loss as to what such an intriguing pair of young people might want with an old man."

His interest suddenly sharpened into suspicion. "Have my children sent you to investigate whether I am on my deathbed? If so, you can tell them the old man has a little more life in him yet, as they would know if they took the time to travel to Wellington to visit."

"We have not come on behalf of your own children, Mr Waterstone," Charlie said, "but on behalf of the children living at Durham House. We understand you have agreed to sell the orphans' home. The matron received an eviction notice only yesterday, effective from tomorrow, Christmas Eve. We have come to plead for an extension to the eviction deadline, if not a halt to the sale."

Gnarled hands plucked at the blanket, lifting it enough for Waterstone to swing his legs around to face them – a slow and obviously agonising process. "You're too late, young man. I have already signed the sale deed."

A woman entered the room with a tray. "Your medicine, Ezra. May I offer your guests tea?" She was a match for Mr Waterstone in looks and age, suggesting a sister or other close relative. Although the woman was free from the arthritis that crippled Mr Waterstone, she moved with the shuffling gait of age.

"Stay a moment, sister," Mr Waterstone said. "Mr Pyke tells me there are orphans being evicted from Durham House at short notice. I am trying to decide whether to hear him out or throw him out of my house for spinning me a sorry tale. What say you, Mr Pyke? Are you trying to buy the place yourself using underhand tactics, or are you simply mistaken?"

"Neither, sir," Charlie said. "I spoke the truth. Miss Penrose was present when Mr Spragg's clerk delivered the eviction notices. Miss Penrose's father, Doctor George Penrose, runs a free medical clinic on

83

the premises and can vouch for the truth of the matter. If you do not believe me, you could come with us now to see for yourself."

"I am an invalid. I have not left this house for many months." Mr Waterstone's steely gaze switched to Grace. "You are Doctor Penrose's daughter?"

"Yes, Mr Waterstone. I can vouch for the truth of Mr Pyke's statements, as can my father."

"I do not know your father personally, but I know he has a fine reputation in the local community. On the other hand, I have known Mr Spragg for many years. Old Mr Spragg, that is, who managed the property since I acquired it as payment for a debt some years ago. I don't know young Mr Spragg well, but if he is his father's son, I can have no reason to doubt his word."

"I do not wish to cast aspersions on a man's character," Grace said, "but I am given to understand that young Mr Spragg is not at all similar to his father. May I ask what he told you about Durham House, sir?"

Mr Waterstone did not speak for several seconds, evidently deciding whether it was in his interests to share confidential information with strangers. "Are you sure the orphans do not wish to leave Durham House?"

"They are eager to stay, sir," Charlie said. "At the very least, they need time to find new premises if they are to be evicted, otherwise the orphans will spend Christmas day without a roof over their heads."

Waterstone's sharp eyes narrowed. "Mr Spragg informed me that Durham House is structurally unsound, such that the orphans' home had given notice and relocated to another building. He showed me a property inspection from a reputable agency to substantiate the claim."

"Would you have sold if you knew the orphans wanted to stay?" Grace asked.

Waterstone considered the question carefully before answering. "I am old, but I am not hard-hearted. I would have discussed the situation with the Durham House Charitable Trust first. However, the truth is that the rents paid to me from the property have dwindled in recent times. I barely cover my costs. With the property in disrepair and my health in decline, I accepted Spragg's advice to sell while a fair offer was on the table."

"To be clear," Charlie said, "Mr Spragg came to you with the suggestion to sell, providing the valuation and property report to you, rather than you approaching him to sell? In addition, he assured you the orphans had moved out?"

"Correct."

"And it is your understanding that the rent was declining?" Charlie continued. "Because the Matron of Durham House, Miss Bentwick, said they are struggling with rent increases."

"Is that so?" Waterstone's wrinkles deepened into a frown. "Marton & Spragg manage the lease on my behalf and have done so, reliably and honourable, for many years. You must think me a fool to believe what I was told, but young Mr Spragg showed me the accounts and provided an independent valuation and inspection from a reputable company. I felt fortunate to sell for the price the buyer is offering in the circumstances. It is a curse to be bedridden and dependent on others. My doctor says I must keep to my bed or the arthritis will get worse."

"If I may be so bold, sir," Grace said, "I must take issue with your doctor. Regular gentle movement is preferable to immobility in such cases. My great-aunt is also afflicted and has made a study of the condition." Before Waterstone could comment on her forthright opinions, Grace gestured to the wheeled chair in the corner of the room. "I see you have a bath chair, Mr Waterstone. Might we take a walk together to Durham House, to give you the chance to see the place for yourself? A little fresh air may not restore your health, but it may make the condition more bearable. Mr Pyke can push the bath chair."

"What about your medicine, Ezra?" his sister said. "Doctor Kent said you must take it regularly. And what of your luncheon?"

Grace had noted the bottle on the tray. "That medicine will only make you sleep away your pain. There are better treatments available. My father, Doctor Penrose, would be delighted to advise you if you wish. As for luncheon, might I suggest you take your midday meal at the soup kitchen the charity runs from Durham House? They provide a hearty meal with the limited means available to them."

Mr Waterstone peered at Grace with the beginnings of a smile. "How could I turn down such a thoughtful offer from a determined young lady? It has been a long time since I had the pleasure of leaving this house. What say you, sister?"

Miss Waterstone cast a dubious eye over the two strangers offering to abduct her brother. "I suppose the day is mild. I have dinner to see to, but I could send our maid to escort you. Better yet, you could wait until your valet returns from his half day."

"I am not a child who needs his hand held," Waterstone declared. "I am sure these young folk will look after me."

Charlie helped Mr Waterstone to stand, while Grace brought over the bath chair. The wheels squeaked with disuse, but the chair moved freely enough and the padding looked comfortable. Grace brushed the dust off and settled the old man with a blanket around his knees, while Charlie went with the sister to find him a hat and scarf.

Within a few minutes, they were out on the street, heading for Durham House. They had to take a longer route, to avoid steps, but their captive showed every sign of enjoying his outing. Mr Waterstone looked less grey in the sunshine of a summer's day. He was soon engaging Grace in a discussion of her great-aunt's recommendations for living with arthritis, many of which were opposed to those of Mr Waterstone's doctor. Before long, the discussion veered onto the good work that Miss Crockett and Miss Bentwick were doing with the orphans and the miserly way Mr Spragg had treated his own employees, as well as his clients.

Mr Waterstone's expression was thoughtful by the time they arrived at Durham House. "There doesn't look to be much wrong with the property from the outside, beyond the need for a lick of paint. What are all these vagrants doing here?"

A line of people stretched from the door down the street. Grace glanced at her pocket watch. "Queuing for the soup kitchen, which is about to open. They come early, because the soup often runs out before all of them can be fed."

One of the men offered to help lift the bath chair up the steps.

"Polite fellow," Waterstone said, once they were inside.

"Sad to say," Grace said, "there are plenty of decent, honest men without work in these troubled times, who would struggle to survive without a hot meal in the middle of the day. Others will have more disreputable pasts, but they cause no bother here. The two men who run the soup kitchen give them a sympathetic welcome, as they were once in the same position." Grace waved to Reaper, who raised tattooed knuckles in reply.

Reaper and Filch were busy lugging enormous pots to the serving area. The aroma filled the hall, the rear of which was set out with tables. While the homeless and destitute entered the hall and took their bowls of soup to the tables, children continued to play and learn at the front of the hall. A pair of older girls were teaching younger girls to sew in one corner, while the boys worked in the opposite corner, constructing wooden footstools. Martha Crockett held up a large card in front of a group of younger children, who were reciting the alphabet after her. Tom waved at Charlie before turning back to his recitation.

The choir was gathering on the stage, ready to begin their midday concert. Miss Bentwick and Reaper were both of the opinion that music nourished the soul, as soup nourished the body. Eva grinned at them from her spot in the front row of the choir. The homeless watched on in silence or chattered quietly. When all the seats at the dining table were taken, the choir started to sing.

Mr Waterstone smiled. "Ah, the sweet sound of children laughing and singing. How I have missed it."

Grace gestured for Miss Bentwick to come over. The matron directed her group of older children to continue their reading – some running their fingers slowly along each line of the book, while others sped through the pages eagerly.

"Mr Waterstone, may I introduce Miss Bentwick, Matron of Durham House Orphans' Home. Mr Waterstone is the owner of this building." Grace held up her hand to stop Miss Bentwick venting her anger. "Mr Waterstone is selling Durham House because the rent monies he receives have been declining and because he was led to believe the orphans had found another home. Mr Waterstone has also been shown a property report that indicates the building is structurally unsound."

"I can see I have been misled as to the orphans, Miss Bentwick," Mr Waterstone acknowledged.

"And regarding the rent," Matron replied. She considered the matter for a moment, then turned to issue her orders. "Miss Crockett, please fetch the account book from my desk. Mr Reaper, may I see you for a moment. Peter Yates, please take over from Mr Reaper at the soup counter."

A tall boy rose from the woodwork group and hurried to the soup counter, passing the soup man on the way. Martha rose from her seat. "You children must sit still and practice being quiet for a moment." She pointed to an older child. "Clementine will read you a story."

Once Reaper had been introduced to Mr Waterstone and the situation explained, he was quick to assist. "You've been sold a crock of lies, Mr Waterstone. I do the maintenance for Durham House and I can tell you the old girl is in fine shape. I was up in the roof space only last month, setting rat traps, and I can tell you there is no dry rot up there. Any leaks in the roof are fixed promptly, rather than waiting an age for the property agent to attend to his duty."

"We had a routine property inspection a few weeks ago," Miss Bentwick added, "but the man did little more than glance around the place and disappear again without a word."

Martha returned with the account books, which she showed to Mr Waterstone. The rent payments were signed off by Matron and Mr Spragg himself.

"I cannot believe it," Mr Waterstone said, after running a gnarled finger down the column of figures with increasing dismay. "You are paying far more than I receive in rent. How greedy you must think me for charging so much. Spragg has some explaining to do. I will be demanding a halt to proceedings until this matter is resolved."

The cluster of adults around Mr Waterstone exchanged delighted smiles and expressed their gratitude.

Behind them, the choir sung the opening notes of "Hark, the Herald Angels Sing". Mr Waterstone closed his eyes and listened. Contentment stole across over his world-weary face, making him appear less grey and more alive. He opened his eyes again and looked around the hall at the children busy with their schooling, while the destitute ate their meal.

When Mr Waterstone spoke again, the sharp edge of anger in his voice was replaced with steely resolve. "In fact, I am not inclined to sell at all. In the circumstances, they cannot force me to honour the contract."

"Especially not as we have the buyer's copy of the sale deed," Charlie said. "We could rip it up now and Mr Holliman would never know that you had signed it. However, I would prefer to keep it as evidence, if that is acceptable to you, Mr Waterstone."

"By all means," Mr Waterstone agreed. "If you pass me the document, I will cross through my signature and add a note withdrawing the offer, just to be on the safe side." Waterstone did so, with painfully slow strokes of the pen. "Now, perhaps Mr Reaper would be so kind as to take me over to the table for a bowl of soup, which smells quite delicious. I should like to speak to a few of the men while I listen to the choir. There is nothing I enjoy more than a choir, except perhaps the music of Chopin."

"I'm more of a Beethoven man myself," Reaper said, as he wheeled Waterstone away. "You ought to meet our Mr Abernathy. He was a pianist of note, before his fingers became too stiff to play. The world had no use for a musician who cannot play, but he finds a warm welcome here."

Reaper soon had Mr Waterstone settled at the end of the table, with Mr Abernathy on one side and Reaper on the other. The two arthritic men held their soup spoons with equal difficulty, but that was soon forgotten as the mismatched trio of men talked of music and the vagaries of life.

Grace could scarcely believe the changes wrought in Mr Waterstone in such a short time. The power of companionship had an amazing ability to dull pain, although she knew Waterstone would suffer for his unaccustomed efforts come evening. As for the outwardly rough Reaper – who knew he was a devotee of classical music? The soft heart underneath his knife-scarred exterior came as no surprise to Grace though, after seeing Reaper tend to the down-at-heel folk who came for their daily meal.

Grace gestured Charlie aside, leaving Martha and Miss Bentwick exchanging teary-eyed embraces.

"What more proof do we need that Spragg is behind this deception?" Grace said.

Charlie's jaw was taunt with anger. "I'd say 'deception' is far too mild a word, Grace. This is outright fraud. At a minimum, Spragg has pocketed a significant proportion of the rent monies from Durham House and either committed forgery or bribed the inspector to prepare a false property report and valuation. Add to that his unconscionable actions towards the orphans and it is fair to say I shall take great pleasure in witnessing his downfall. I am only sorry that Spragg's demise will affect your brother and Mr Crockett."

"They will recover," Grace said. "Spragg cannot be allowed to get away with his crimes. What are we waiting for? Let's take the matter to the police."

Charlie held her back with a hand on her arm. "Wait, Grace. I believe there is more to be uncovered. For one thing, Spragg has been acting strangely." He told her what Eva had seen when she peered into Spragg's house last night.

"Eva thought she saw a dead person and coffins?" Grace shivered. "Haven't we investigated enough suspicious deaths for one year? Eva must be mistaken. Even if she did see a corpse, it might be a family bereavement, which might also explain Spragg's absence from his business."

"I hope you're right, but Jake told me that Mr Spragg has no family or friends. I want to have a look at Spragg's house for myself. I'd like to talk to him too, before we take the matter to the police. It seems to me that Mr Holliman is the one who has the most to gain from the low price he is paying for Durham House. Spragg only gains if Holliman is in on the swindle and willing to reward Spragg for his deception."

"You think they are in it together?" Grace asked. "That makes sense. How would we prove it, if Spragg was the one who commissioned the fraudulent reports? Holliman has only to say he was an innocent party and he will get away with it."

"Maybe he would, in this was the only case. But your mother said that Holliman was known for buying up houses cheaply. What if they have pulled this swindle before, possibly many times? The Durham House fraud relied on Waterstone being too incapacitated to know what was really going on. Presumably, if there are other victims, they would also have been targeted because they were vulnerable. I would

91

very much like to know how Holliman and Spragg knew which victims to swindle."

"Spragg might know that Mr Waterstone was ill," Grace said, "because he was the leasing agent for Durham House. However, my mother told me of an acquaintance who sold to Holliman Construction after her husband had died, when she was desperate to sell. What did my mother say? 'The poor man was on his deathbed when Spragg came knocking on her door. He didn't even wait until he was cold in the ground.' The way she said it implied the acquaintance did not know Spragg – he just appeared at the very moment she needed to sell."

"If Spragg pressured a woman to sell her home when her husband was on his deathbed," Charlie said, "he must be a man entirely without conscience. The question is, how would he know the man was about to die and the wife was desperate to sell?"

"Spragg or Holliman might have a contact who knows when people are gravely ill. A doctor, for example, or a nurse. I know Mr Waterstone's doctor is Doctor Kent from the inscription on his medicine bottle. I shall pay Doctor Kent a visit while you go to Spragg's house."

"Take your father with you, Grace. Doctor Kent will be more willing to talk to another doctor. And ask your mother for the name of her friend and any other people she knows who have sold to Holliman. I'll meet you at the offices of Marton & Spragg as soon as I can. Jake said Mr Spragg will return around three o'clock this afternoon, so we must hurry."

Grace reached up to kiss Charlie's cheek. "I'll get Reaper to take Mr Waterstone home. They seem to be enjoying each other's company immensely. Look, young Tom is with them too, talking about who knows what."

"He's a bright child, as is his sister," Charlie said. "Those poor children have been through a great deal, but I rather think Tom and Eva are going to do just fine in their new home."

For Whom The Bell Tolls

The bells of St Paul's church chimed twice as Grace hurried back to her home, hoping that her mother and father would be there. They were. Better yet, her parents knew the names of three local families who had sold properties to Holliman Construction under distressing circumstances. None were patients of her father. As there were only two general practice doctors in the area, Grace surmised they attended Doctor Kent's surgery.

Doctor Penrose refused to accept that his fellow practitioner could be passing confidential patient information to Mr Spragg. He accompanied Grace to Doctor Kent's surgery reluctantly, arguing that Spragg must have another means of identifying seriously ill or incapacitated owners who might be convinced to sell desirable properties. Indeed, Grace suspected her father only came with her to stop her from offending his colleague.

In the end, the visit to Doctor Kent's surgery was far quicker than Grace had expected. She and her father had scarcely stepped over the threshold into the reception area when the truth became apparent. The man who greeted them from behind the reception desk was the spitting image of Mr Holliman, except for his lack of a handlebar moustache. He was also a generation younger and far less skilled in the art of deflecting questions.

Grace got straight to the point. "Good afternoon," she said brightly. "Goodness me, you must be the son of Mr Theodore Holliman. How alike you look! I had the honour of conversing with your father recently. What a difference he has made to the city. You must be proud."

The young man reddened and looked around to see if there was a corner he might escape into, but there was nowhere to hide. "Mr Holliman is my uncle, not my father." His eyes darted sideways again. "In truth, I do not know him well, as my family are looked upon as the poor relations. How may I assist you today, Miss –?"

"Oh, dear me, look at the time," Grace twittered. "I must have my schedule of engagements in a muddle again. I shall have to return another time."

She herded her bemused father towards the door, but not before noting that the young man had a gold watch hanging out of the pocket of his expensive brocade waistcoat, leaving little doubt that the poor relation had found a way to make his way up in the world. Charlie had been right. Holliman and Spragg were in this swindle together and would stop at nothing to acquire properties cheaply, even if it meant stealing confidential patient information.

Doctor Penrose hurried after her along the street. "Grace, dear, I'm not at all sure that I care for your skill in the art of subterfuge. Can you not leave the investigating to Charlie?"

"Would you rather have the orphans sleeping on the street on Christmas Day, Papa?"

"Well, no, of course not … but … well, I don't think your mother would approve."

Dear sweet father, Grace thought, hoping he would never change. She decided not to enlighten him as to his wife's expertise in graciously and subtly bending people to her will. How did her father imagine her mother succeeded at raising money for the various charities she supported, let alone her impressive performance in Holliman's office this morning?

"Mother would be on the orphans' side too, I expect," was all Grace said on the matter. "I must be going. I will see you this evening."

Quarter of an hour later, Grace reached the premises of Marton & Spragg.

Jake rushed to greet her as soon as the bell on the door heralded her arrival. "Oh, it's you, Grace. I was hoping it would be Charlie, bringing back the stolen property file. Did you hear the news? We were burgled last night."

"Charlie told me," Grace replied. "Given his exceptional skills as a detective, you will not be surprised to hear that Charlie found the stolen documents this morning. However, they are no longer needed. The owner of Durham House no longer wishes to sell."

Jake advanced on her, his face tight with irritation. "Grace, what have you been up to behind my back? I will lose my position here if Mr Spragg finds out you have pestered a client into changing his mind on a sale. Besides, the owner cannot withdraw from the deal after he has signed the deeds."

Grace didn't budge. "Frankly, Jake, losing your position is the least of your worries. Mr Spragg and Mr Holliman are defrauding property owners by using false valuations, fake property reports, and confidential medical information. It's time we made a thorough search of your employer's office to find out the extent of his crimes."

"No! That cannot be true." Jake stepped in front of Spragg's office door, barring the way. "Grace, I refuse to let you in. When Mr Spragg arrives, I will let Charlie put his evidence forward and allow Mr Spragg an opportunity to refute the allegations."

Mr Crockett handed his set of keys to Grace. "I beg your pardon, Mr Penrose, but I would rather risk Mr Spragg's ire than allow him to get away with his misdeeds." He nodded to an envelope on his desk. "I have already prepared my letter of resignation, after the shameful way he tried to evict the orphans. I shall serve out the required notice if required, naturally. If I am fortunate, it will be enough time to allow me to find a new position."

Jake wavered, but not for long. "You are right, Mr Crockett. Honour before self-interest. I apologise, Grace. I will conduct the search while you remain here."

Grace allowed Jake to search, for the sake of his honour. He emerged ten minutes later with several files of property sales to Holliman Construction. While Jake and Mr Crockett examined the files, Grace took the opportunity to slip into Spragg's office. Her brother might be a good land agent, but he had no idea how to conduct a proper search. She was under the desk, prodding the cracks of what might be a hidden compartment, when Jake's footsteps returned.

"Pray tell, sister, why are you on your hands and knees underneath the furniture? Need I point out that the drawers are on the outside of the desk?"

"Very droll, Jake." Grace found the hidden catch and crawled out from beneath Spragg's desk, bottom first, catching one of her gown's ruffles on a sharp edge. She stood up and shook the dust off her gown, which was no longer as pristine as it had been this morning. "You have no imagination, brother. No wonder you always lost at hide-and-seek and I always won."

Jake rolled his eyes. "How does it feel to be marrying the most elegant lady in the country, Charlie? You can see why her mother gave up on dressing her in pretty white dresses."

Charlie was leaning on the door frame, a valise at his feet, and his almond eyes stretched with amusement. "I refuse to answer on the grounds that it might be incriminating." He dropped a file onto the desk. "Here are the sale documents, Jake."

Jake grabbed the file. "I'm in your debt, Charlie. How on earth did you find the stolen documents so quickly? I will never question your detective skills again." He cast a mischievous glance at his sister. "A pity your future wife is not as skilled at finding hidden documents."

Grace pulled out the sliding panel she had unlocked under the desk. A ledger and more files crammed the hidden drawer. Jake had the grace to blush. Charlie simply smiled and kept his mouth shut.

"Are you going to tell me who the burglar was?" Jake asked, in an obvious attempt to change the subject. When Charlie didn't reply, Jake sighed. "Was it Martha, after all? I beg you, do not tell the police. I'm sure she did it out of the goodness of her sweet heart and not for her own gain."

"The police need never know the documents were missing," Charlie agreed. "You were right about the burglar having a good heart and pure motive, Jake, but I can assure you that it wasn't Martha Crockett."

"I knew it. It was the tattooed soup man."

Grace closed the door to the office, so Mr Crockett could not overhear her. "Jake, why are you being such an idiot? You obviously admire Martha and she is the perfect woman for you, although far better than you deserve. Yet, still you fail to tell her your feelings."

Jake crossed his arms over his chest. "Do you expect me to thank you for your unsolicited advice, sister? As it happens, I chose not to have my head turned by her merits. I don't want to be a junior employee in a failing land agency forever, Grace. I need to marry well in order to buy my own business and get on in the world."

Grace knew Jake was clever, but sometimes he could also be impossibly foolish. "Love is far more important than riches, Jake. Besides, you have all the skills and intelligence you need to make your own way in the world. You must simply start a rung or two lower and work your way up."

"I know I've been a fool, Grace, but it is too late now. If this ledger shows Spragg is committing fraud, my reputation will go down with his."

Grace held out the ledger. "Better to know the truth, Jake, especially when you're innocent of any wrongdoing. Besides, if Spragg is charged with fraud, you might be able to buy this agency for next to nothing."

"I will do what is right, whatever the consequences." Jake opened the office door. "Mr Crockett, may I have you in here, please? We have some accounts to decipher."

Mr Crockett entered the office so quickly, he must have been waiting by the door for the call. He was soon seated at Spragg's desk, going through the ledger and scribbling addition sums and long division workings on a piece of paper. Not ten minutes passed before the mild, unassuming Mr Crockett was thumping the desk and frothing at the mouth. Jake was as pale as a ghost.

"Sinful, appalling deception," Mr Crockett railed. "Dear old Mr Spragg and Mr Marton would be rolling in their graves at this desecration of their honest reputations. I suggest we call the constabulary without further ado."

Grace laid a calming hand on his shoulder. "May we know what you have discovered, Mr Crockett?"

Mr Crockett took up the ledger and showed them a page of figures. "Here are the rent payments received for Durham House and the rent forwarded to the owner, Mr Waterstone." He cleared his throat to stifle the tremor in his voice. "Spragg has been withholding an exorbitant percentage of rents as a commission fee. A few percent would be standard business practice, but my calculations show he had taken a third of the rent monies for himself."

"You can see why Mr Waterstone wanted to sell Durham House," Jake said. "The rent he was receiving would hardly cover his costs."

Mr Crockett flipped the pages of the ledger. "The property sales are the same. Spragg was being paid an outrageous commission on the sale of properties to Holliman Construction. Thus, he was making more than twice the usual fee, despite the grossly undervalued sale prices."

Grace was leafing through the papers in the file that she had found with the ledger. "I'm afraid it gets worse, Jake." She handed over a letter. "Here's proof that Spragg and Holliman have been bribing a valuer to falsify the condition and value of properties."

"Outright fraud, without a shadow of a doubt. Mr Crockett is right. We must summon the police immediately."

Grace stopped flipping through the papers in the file. The document that had caught her attention felt like a red-hot coal in her hand. "Er, Jake, you might want to see this first."

"I'm not sure I want to hear any more," Jake groaned. "What is it, Grace?"

"Deeds for the sale of this building to Holliman Construction. Already signed by Spragg and Holliman, with the ownership having passed to Holliman last week. Spragg was given dispensation to stay in the former premises of Marton & Spragg until this afternoon at five o'clock."

If Jake had been pale before, now he turned to the hue and immobility of marble.

Mr Crockett was a man punched in the gut. "Marton & Spragg has been sold? Quarter of a century I have worked for this company for a pittance, and this is how Spragg repays my loyalty? Cast out without warning or a fair period of notice? With Martha and I both out of work, we will be destitute. There is no chance of either of us finding a new position over the Christmas period."

This notion galvanised Jake. "I will not allow your family to suffer, Mr Crockett. That I solemnly swear. Spragg may have sunk to the depths of disgraceful behaviour, but the Penrose family holds higher standards."

Grace's heart swelled with pride at her brother's reaction. Before she could commend him, Charlie interrupted. "Unfortunately, there is something else I need to tell you about Spragg. I went to his house, after Eva told us of evil doings –"

Behind them, the mantlepiece clock chimed three times. Outside, the city's church and town bells also struck thrice. The slight discrepancy in their timings created a discordant ringing in the ears.

The bell on the front door tinkled and footsteps crossed the threshold, accompanied by an odd squeaking, as of a little-used wheel turning.

99

Resolutions

Charlie went to see who had entered the outer office. He had been expecting Spragg, but the new arrivals were Martha and Mr Waterstone, with Reaper pushing the bath chair.

"We have come to seek justice," Mr Waterstone said. "Is Spragg here?"

"Not yet," Charlie replied. "Come in and meet Mr Penrose and Mr Crockett, who are helping us gather the growing mass of evidence proving that Mr Spragg and Mr Holliman were engaged in a widespread campaign of fraud."

No sooner were the introductions made than the bell tinkled again. A tall, hollow-cheeked man entered, his face as pale as the ghoul Eva thought she had seen in Spragg's house. Charlie noted his broad shoulders and rough hands, more suited to a tradesman than a land agent, but knew this man was Mr Spragg from the way Jake Penrose and Mr Crockett stiffened their spines when they saw him.

"What the devil is going on here?" Spragg barked. "Who are you people?" His gaze dropped to the man in the bath chair. "Why, Mr Waterstone, forgive me. I did not expect to see you here."

"You have some explaining to do, Mr Spragg," Waterstone said. "I demand the sale be rescinded immediately. You have cruelly deceived me regarding the state of Durham House and defrauded me of rent monies as well."

Jake Penrose held up the ledger Grace had found in the secret desk drawer. "You have brought shame on your father's fine reputation, Mr Spragg. Stealing from Mr Waterstone and the orphans, taking bribes and falsifying documents for your own pecuniary gain. This is a matter for the police."

100

Spragg quailed at the sight of the ledger. "You had no right to enter my office, Penrose. I warn you, if you call the police, I will drag you down with me." Spragg darted forward, trying to wrest the ledger from Jake's hand.

Charlie placed his solid bulk between the two men. "Durham House will not be sold, Mr Spragg, and these documents are required as evidence in the fraud case I am investigating in my capacity as a detective."

Spragg took one look at Charlie and turned tail. Reaper stepped in front of Spragg, cutting off his path to the exit. "You owe these fine folks an explanation, Mr Spragg."

Spragg retreated, sinking into the chair by his clerk's desk and covering his eyes.

"You cheated everyone," Jake said. "You lived the life of a rich man, while defrauding our clients and giving Mr Crockett and I the impression the business was struggling, so we would work harder for less pay. And now you have the gall to sell Marton & Spragg without having the decency to warn us in advance. I could have bought the business off you for the paltry price you sold it to Holliman, if only I'd known. Nothing will give me greater pleasure than to see you arrested for your wrongdoings."

"You do not understand," Spragg groaned. "I am no criminal."

Reaper snorted. "No, you're worse. No self-respecting criminal would cheat the poor for their own gain. I should know. I've stolen many a silver candlestick from wealthy homes in my past, but I would never be so dishonourable as to steal bread from mouths of desperate men, as you did when you cheated us of funds for the soup kitchen."

"I am running a business, not a charity," Spragg mumbled.

"Don't try to pass off your grasping ways as canny business dealing," Jake interrupted. "Taking such a huge cut of the profits is not an honest commission fee, it is disgraceful and dishonest."

101

Martha Crockett swept to the front of the group, pushing back her blonde curls and wearing an expression of such righteousness that she needed no scales or sword to be Lady Justice.

"A business should provide an honest service to the benefit of society, rather than draining it like a leech, Mr Spragg," Martha declared. "Did you never think of those you hurt? Of the orphans, living hand to mouth thanks to the charity of decent folk, not being able to afford books and pencils, or coal in the winter. You have almost driven my family to the poorhouse with your miserly ways since your father's death. Your dear, kind father would be ashamed of what his son has become. How can you live with yourself when you take advantage of honest men like Mr Waterstone, who was bedridden and unable to protect himself against your lies?"

Mr Waterstone may have been an elderly invalid this morning, but now he sat in the bath chair with the dignity of a general astride his charger. In contrast, Spragg's body curled into a hedgehog's defence.

"It is even worse than that, Martha," Grace said. "Spragg and Holliman deliberately targeted vulnerable people in their disgraceful scheme to get rich. Mr Holliman has a nephew working in a doctor's surgery, who must have passed on information about people who were incapacitated or dying. Deliberately targeting the vulnerable for financial gain is as low as a man can go, don't you think, Mr Spragg? Have you no shame?"

Spragg raised his head at last. His voice, when it finally came, trembled with anguish. "It's true. I thought only of myself. I see that now and regret what I have done, although at the time it seemed as if I had no other option." Spragg darted a glance at his father's portrait on the wall, before looking away just as quickly. "Holliman had me over a barrel. I beg you, do not take this matter to the police. I would rather die than be locked inside a cell."

"It is no more than you deserve," Waterstone said, "but I agree that incarceration serves little purpose. My idea of justice is that victims

102

receive fair recompense for their suffering and the perpetrator learns a hard lesson in how to treat decent folk."

A flicker of hope uncurled Spragg's spine. "I will do whatever you ask. I am not made for this life." He waved his hand around the office. "I never wanted to be a land agent, but my father insisted I take on the business when he became ill. I wanted to travel to Europe, to visit the great galleries of the world, to be my own man."

"To learn to sculpt under the masters, I suppose," Charlie said. "I have visited your house and seen the statues you have crafted. You have talent, but that does not excuse your disgraceful attempt to abandon your life here for the life you would prefer in Europe. You could have paid for a lifetime of travel if you had sold the house you inherited from your father, without resorting to dishonesty. But that is not the path you chose, was it, Mr Spragg?"

Spragg opened his mouth to argue, but clamped it shut again when he saw the valise in Charlie's hand.

Charlie opened the valise, revealing a stack of banknotes and bearer bonds. A passenger ticket sat on top. "This valise contains your ill-gotten gains and a ticket on a ship sailing to London tonight. When I visited your house, I found your possessions packed into trunks, and your precious sculptures and furniture covered with dust-cloths. The evidence could not be clearer, Mr Spragg. You not only committed fraud, but you planned to abandon your employees, having already sold your business. Fleeing your troubles is a coward's way out."

"You had no right to search my home or steal my money," Spragg countered, but the contempt in the faces surrounding him rendered the words feeble. He shrank from the circle of accusing eyes. "I know it was not honourable, but I had no choice – none at all. I know you will not believe me when I say I never meant to defraud anyone."

"Pray tell," Waterstone said. "Every accused man deserves the chance to explain his actions."

"It was all Holliman's doing. I know that sounds like an excuse, but it is the truth. Holliman approached me after my father died and offered me an excellent fee for negotiating a property sale on his behalf. All I had to do was tip the deal in his favour by adjusting the property valuation by a small amount. It was a trap. He told me I could be arrested if I did not continue to help him. He wanted more and more, never letting me out of his clutches, no matter how I pleaded with him."

"You cannot deny he paid you well for your deception," Jake said.

"Yes, but it was only a fraction of the money Holliman made from the deals. His apparent generosity was merely a lure to drag me deeper into his schemes. When Holliman wanted to buy Marton & Spragg, to tear the building down for redevelopment, I saw the chance to escape. What could I do but agree to the paltry price he offered? All I wanted was to take the money and disappear to the far side of the world, so I never had to see him or his thugs again. Please, I beg you, arrest Holliman if you must, but let me go. I will leave tonight and never darken your doors again."

"Why should we believe you, after all the lies you have told?" Jake asked.

"Because I have already written a full confession." Spragg took a letter from his pocket. "I intended to post it to you, Mr Penrose, right before my ship departed. Read it if you wish. The letter details the entirety of Holliman's schemes and tells you where I was going to leave the ledgers and files as proof. You have those already, of course, but the letter still demonstrates my intention to make a clean slate of my dealings, so Holliman could be brought to justice."

Charlie took the letter and read it. "This will go a long way towards convicting Mr Holliman of fraud, alongside the documentation and other evidence we have gathered."

"You will note that the letter also exonerates my employees from any wrongdoing," Spragg said. "Mr Holliman is due to meet me here at five o'clock to collect the signed sale deeds for Durham House and the keys for this building. You could arrest him then. All I ask is that you take pity on me and let me go."

Mr Waterstone interrupted. "You ask too much, Spragg. Justice must be served by you as well as Holliman. Your confession is to be commended, but you still planned to leave with the proceeds of your crimes. That money belongs to your victims, not you."

"I will gladly pay you back the rent money I took, Mr Waterstone." Spragg grabbed the valise from Charlie and pulled out a bundle of banknotes, thrusting them at Waterstone.

"This will go to the Durham House Charitable Trust," Waterstone said, "for it is the charity you cheated, as well as me. The orphans deserve a little Christmas cheer, I'm sure you will agree." He handed the money to Spragg's clerk. "I would be grateful if you would you check this against the amount owed in overpaid rent, Mr Crockett."

"With pleasure, sir." Crockett referred to the sums he had done earlier, before counting the notes in the bundle with nimble fingers. Two more bundles of notes were liberated from the valise before he was satisfied. "By my calculations, that takes care of the matter of the stolen rent monies."

Mr Waterstone was not finished. "We still have the matter of the sums defrauded from the people whose properties you sold based on wrongful valuations or their own desperation to sell because of illness or infirmity. All of it must be repaid to those who lost by your unscrupulous dealings."

Spragg gasped. "All of it?"

"I insist upon it," Waterstone said, "if you wish to avoid having your role in the fraud revealed to the police before your ship sails. Of course, your complicity will come out eventually, making a return to this country inadvisable."

"It will take a considerable period of time to make an accurate calculation of the amounts defrauded," Mr Crockett said. "The true value of the properties must first be ascertained, before the extent of the fraud can be determined. I expect Mr Holliman took the lion's share."

"Can you estimate approximately how much Spragg made by the deceit?" Charlie asked.

Crockett went back to his jottings, arriving at a figure and placing it, with evident pleasure, in front of his employer. Spragg gagged at the amount, but made no further comment as Mr Waterstone directed Mr Crockett to remove the stated amount in bundles of banknotes and bonds from the rapidly dwindling supply in the valise.

"Will you not leave me a little to live on?" Spragg pleaded.

"You are still wealthier than most hard-working men, Mr Spragg," Jake said. "A dedicated artist will not need much to live on."

When the clerk finished his redistribution of funds, Mr Waterstone gave a satisfied nod. His previously grey complexion had taken on a decidedly rosy hue. "Well, ladies and gentlemen, shall we let Mr Spragg have his chance to flee?"

"Not yet," Grace said. "There is another injustice to rectify. Mr Crockett and my brother have been cruelly underpaid this past year and are now out of work without notice. What do you say to a Christmas bonus to right the wrong?"

"I like the sound of it very much," Jake said. "Do as my dear sister says, Mr Crockett."

Mr Crockett looked to Mr Waterstone for his agreement.

Waterstone was quick to assent. "Do as Miss Penrose suggests, my good sir. Your lovely daughter apprised me of the full situation as we made our way to Marton & Spragg. You deserve every penny."

Spragg had given up his protestations, although seeing his wealth vanish before his eyes brought tears to his eyes. He sunk into his chair, an object of misery. "I shall be penniless at this rate."

"You could sell your house," Charlie suggested.

"I am leaving tonight," Spragg reminded him. "Who would buy my house at such short notice?"

"I shall purchase it," Waterstone said. "I expect to receive a discount on the true value equivalent to the amount you would have duped me out of on the sale of Durham House. Mr Penrose, perhaps you would be so good as to draw up the sale documents?"

"Certainly, Mr Waterstone. It would be my pleasure." Jake hastened to his cubicle and took up his pen with relish.

"Mr Crockett," Waterstone said, "I shall need a tenant for my new house. I wonder if your family would consider taking it on? I can assure you the rent will be very reasonable, as I am sure you will take good care of the property. You will need a larger home now that you have those two charming orphans added to your household. I must say, I envy you, having Miss Eva singing in your home every day. And young Master Tom seems a lively lad."

Mr Crockett was incapable of speech at the rapid turn of events in his favour. Martha spoke for him. "We accept your kind offer, Mr Waterstone, with deepest gratitude. We hope you will visit us there often and dine with us. Perhaps Mr Penrose might join us too?"

"I would be delighted, Miss Crockett," Jake replied from his desk. "With my extra wages and my savings, I plan to lease an office and start my own land agency. I would be honoured, Mr Crockett, if you would join me in that enterprise. As a clerk, if you wish, although I would prefer a partnership." Jake glanced around the gloomy office. "I suggest we lease a lighter room with happier memories."

Mr Crocket was still speechless, so Martha again took the initiative. "What a splendid idea, Mr Penrose. I know Mr Spragg has a large house. Perhaps we might use a portion of it as the premises for the business, so that Mr Waterstone gains an extra amount of rent for his generosity. 'Penrose & Crockett' has a fine ring to it, does it not?"

Jake beamed at her. "So it does, Miss Crockett, so it does. For the rest of today, I shall be busy with paperwork. Tomorrow, however, I will be temporarily out of work. I wonder if you would care to take a stroll with me, if that would be permitted?"

Martha caught the eye of her father, who nodded. "I would enjoy that very much, Mr Penrose."

"An excellent result all around," Grace said. "Are we agreed that Mr Spragg has fully recompensed his victims?" When all present nodded, she continued. "He has also provided the means to bring justice to the main offender in this case, Mr Holliman. What do we think? Does Mr Spragg deserve our charity so close to Christmas? Shall we let him follow his dream of becoming a sculptor, now that he has learned his lesson and paid his debt?"

After a brief discussion, it was agreed that Spragg could go, once all the calculations had been confirmed, and the documents signed. Once Spragg left, they would call the police to arrest Holliman.

Charlie was as stunned as Spragg at this rapid dispensing of justice. "May I suggest that Jake Penrose and Mr Crockett alert the police, rather than me. They must get the full credit for uncovering the fraud, to ensure they are not under suspicion of collusion, as Mr Spragg's employees. Miss Penrose and I will fade away, as if we were never here."

Grave Matters

Grace felt her spirits lift still further when she and Charlie were back out on the street in the sunshine. "I'm glad that's over. I had feared that Mr Spragg would turn out to be a lunatic as well as a fraudster, after Eva's description of his house."

Charlie took her arm and led her away at such a rapid pace, she knew that he too was glad to see the last of Spragg. He slowed again when they reached the bustle of the main street. "I'm not surprised Eva was scared," Charlie said, as they waited to cross the road. "Even in daylight, Spragg's sculptures looked ghostly covered by dust-cloths. In the dim light of dusk, they must have looked terrifying. If it hadn't been for Eva and Tom, I would never have visited the house and realised Spragg's intention to flee with the money."

"Are you satisfied with Mr Waterstone's version of justice for Mr Spragg?"

"I am. Spragg was naïve to accept commissions from Holliman, but I believe him when he said he never intended to be caught up in such a large-scale fraud. Of course, he should have gone to the police immediately, but at least his victims will be compensated."

It had been a close call, Grace thought. Spragg could so easily have escaped, leaving the orphans homeless. "All's well that ends well, as the bard would have us believe."

"Indeed, it all ended much more happily than I expected," Charlie said. "Even Mr Spragg ought to be content that he will realise his dream, albeit without the riches he wished for. Far better than a life within the grim walls of a cell, as his partner in crime will find out. Spragg should count himself lucky to be gone when Holliman finds out he has been tricked by a man he thought he had in his power."

"I am relieved we will not be there when the police arrest Holliman."

"Would you care to take that long-promised walk in the Botanical Gardens, Grace, now that our work is done?"

"A walk would be lovely," Grace agreed, "but our work is far from done, Charlie. The most important crime of all is yet to be solved."

Charlie stopped to buy flowers from a woman on a street corner, making her day by buying three extravagant bunches. They resumed their walk, surrounded by blooms, attracting smiles from passers-by. After a time, Charlie spoke again. "What crime is yet to be solved, Grace?"

"My stolen engagement ring, of course. Christmas Eve is tomorrow. We cannot let Jake win the bet."

Charlie lapsed into silence again, but Grace was not of a mind to hold back her thoughts. "If Jake had any honour at all, he would give my ring back. After all you have done for him today, when you could have been searching the house for the ring."

"Jake offered to return the ring," Charlie admitted, "but I turned him down. I did not wish him to think he had won, as I would never live it down."

"I understand the sentiment, but the ring must be well hidden or we would have found it by now. It is hopeless."

"I wouldn't say that. Jake hinted that the hiding place related to what you enjoy about Christmas."

"A great help that is, since I love everything about Christmas." Grace hadn't been taking much notice of where they were going, but now she saw they were approaching the gates of the Bolton Street Cemetery, with the sexton's cottage beyond. "Oh, what a nice idea. We can walk through the cemetery to the Botanical Gardens. Did you know we have a family plot here?"

Charlie smiled the enigmatic smile that always made Grace's heart turn flips. "What did you think the flowers were for, my darling? We need to pay a visit to your grandmother to thank her for all she has done. I've begun to think of her as the Ghost of Christmas Past, although a loving ghost, not a frightening one."

Grace did not know what Charlie was talking about. She glanced at the flowers, noting irises, roses and lilies.

He read her mind. "Irises for your grandmother, roses and lilies for your sisters, Rosemary and Lily. I wasn't sure what to get for your grandfather, but I expect he won't mind sharing the irises."

Charlie's thoughtfulness melted Grace to the core. She said no more as she guided him along a winding route between grand and humble headstones, on a path lined with trees and flowers. They reached the family plot, where her grandparents lay side by side, together forever as they had been in life. Her sisters, who had died too young, were at their side. Grace put the flowers in the waiting pots, brightening up their graves for Christmas.

When Grace had had her fill of silent contemplation, Charlie knelt before her. "In front of your grandparents, who loved you so much, and your sisters, lost too young, I ask you again to marry me, Grace Penrose, and be mine forever."

Grace did not trust herself to speak when she saw he held her engagement ring in his hand. He removed her glove and slipped the ring onto her finger. Grace hadn't been so overcome with emotion since the day he first proposed.

She slid her fingers between his, relishing the familiar press of the ring into her skin, held tight against his hand. "Thank you, my darling. I felt lost without my ring. And yes, I will marry you. I could not even begin to contemplate life without you."

"Walk with me, my love," Charlie whispered.

They walked up the hill and found a seat in a secluded spot in the Botanical Gardens. Grace nestled into his arms. "You have been here for little more than a day, Charlie, and you have uncovered a fraud, solved a burglary, rescued the orphans' home, and found my ring. Quite an accomplishment, even by your standards."

Charlie inhaled a deep breath of air warmed by the sun and perfumed with flowers. "We did it together, with the help of your family, your grandmother's spirit, two inquisitive orphans, a clever burglar, and a bedridden gentleman. Not exactly the traditional Christmas holiday I had expected, but diverting nevertheless."

"I'm not convinced that mystery solving should be added to our list of Penrose Christmas traditions, but at least we completed the investigation without the risk of bodily harm, which makes a pleasant change." Grace felt the muscles of Charlie's arm tighten around her and regretted her careless choice of words.

"Not entirely without risk, Grace, as you might have been caught when you broke into Spragg's office or attacked while roaming the city streets in the dead of night."

Grace had been wondering when that little issue would be broached. She regretted not telling Charlie before she burgled Spragg's office, but she hadn't wanted to risk him spending his first Penrose Christmas in a police cell. Grace decided to side-step the issue. "Jake was astonished you solved the burglary at all, considering the dearth of clues."

"The lack of clues was your downfall, Grace. No burglar would have been half so careful. A rock through the pane of glass would have been a far more typical method."

"I hoped Jake would not notice that he had been burgled. I wanted him to believe that he had merely mislaid the sale documents for Durham House."

"I would have been content to leave it at that," Charlie said, "except that Jake was positive the papers had been stolen and fixed on Martha as the villain. Don't worry, Grace, Jake will never know it was you. I threw him off the scent with a plausible explanation for how the burglar entered."

Grace tucked her head against his shoulder, enjoying the weight of his arm around her. How many other men would remain this calm while discuss their future wife's criminal endeavours? "I was expecting you to keelhaul me for taking such a risk."

His arm lifted, as if he was about to withdraw it from her shoulders, probably so he could cross it over his chest for the inevitable lecture. But the arm dropped back into place, pulling her closer. "Would there be any point? I have asked you before to inform me in advance of any risky ventures, with no discernible effect. I can only suppose that you didn't wish to compromise my relationship with my future brother-in-law in this instance."

"You know me too well, Charlie. Am I becoming too predictable?"

"Grace Penrose, the day you become predictable is the day I retire in glory. I may admire your courage, but I am still appalled that you went into the city alone in the dark to commit a crime."

Charlie paused to examine her face. "Oh, I see. You didn't go alone."

"I'm not totally reckless," Grace admitted. "Reaper escorted me and stood guard at the entrance to the lane. I know I should have told you, but you would have insisted on doing it yourself."

"Marvellous." Charlie forced the word out through gritted teeth. "I feel so much better knowing that you chose the help of a hardened criminal over your future husband."

"A reformed criminal," Grace corrected. "Reaper insisted on helping me to save the orphans' home and his soup kitchen. I wanted to ask for your help, but I had a vision of you being bailed out of custody by your future father-in-law. I simply couldn't risk that humiliation."

Charlie exhaled a long, slow lung-full of air. "I suppose I should be grateful to have found a wife who cares more for my safety than her own."

Grace didn't push her luck. Time to change the subject. "What clues gave me away?"

"I noticed your boots by the back door this morning, when I went out early."

"My boots?" Grace prompted, slipping her arm around his waist.

"Evidently, from the damp and trace of mud, you had been out even earlier than me. Before daylight, in fact, judging by the splash of candle-wax on one boot. The reason became clear when Jake told me the documents were missing. Of the few people with motive, and even fewer with knowledge of the whereabouts of the file, who else would open the window with such surgical precision? Who else had been standing by the window the previous afternoon and thus had the opportunity to open the sash lock? Despite the care you took, you stepped in a patch of grime, leaving enough of a mark for me to recognise the familiar boot print. All in all, it was elementary, my dear Grace."

"Charlie Pyke, sometimes your investigative talents terrify me. How fortunate that I am marrying you, so you cannot testify against me in any future transgressions."

Charlie rested his cheek against hers. "As if I would, when your talents are essential to my success. You also left a fragment of wool on a splinter of wood. The wool gave me a moment's doubt, as I had noted earlier in the day that Martha's skirt had a loose hem. I borrowed George's microscope to see if I could distinguish one sample of wool from another. That is the most fascinating part of all. Did you know that the dark grey wool from your skirt has a fine strand of dark green visible under magnification? The wool from the sash lock was identical, quite unlike several other samples I tried, even though the yarns looked almost indistinguishable to the eye."

114

"Fascinating, I'm sure. I suppose you want to purchase a microscope now."

"I will have other priorities, once I have a wife to fend for." Charlie gave her a smile that sent her pulse on a merry dance. "I expect your constant demands for ladylike fripperies will leave me destitute before long. New bonnets and bows and ribbons. Pretty white gowns with ruffles and puffed sleeves. Jemmies and lock picks and weaponry."

"Very amusing, Charlie. You know I have everything I require already." Grace took off her glove to admire her ring again, back where it belonged. "You haven't told me when and where you found my ring."

"I found it this morning, but I wanted to wait for the right moment to return it to you. Your dear departed grandmother gave me the clue during a dream."

Grace started to laugh, but stopped when Charlie did not join in. "You cannot be serious, Charlie. Grandma Penrose came to you in a dream to tell you where Jake had hidden my ring? What will your business partner say when I tell him of your unorthodox detection methods? Will you be consulting a crystal ball and tarot cards next, my dear?"

"All I know is that I woke up with the absolute certainty that your grandmother had spoken to me. Call if a vision or a visitation, if you believe such things, or put it down to the unconscious workings of the mind, but it led me straight to the ring, with the help of your Aunt Sophie and Jake himself. I'll explain later, after we have had a little fun at your brother's expense for doubting my abilities."

"I like the sound of that. Jake should be made to pay dearly for taking my ring and calling your detecting talents into question. What did you have in mind? Another haunting? Perhaps Grandma Penrose's ghost could be persuaded to join the fun. She always had a fine sense of humour."

Charlie whispered in her ear. Grace chuckled. "Charlie Pyke, that is so very wicked, I wish I had thought of it myself." Grace nudged him with her elbow. "Now, about that walk you promised me. I know of a hidden path, where we might take a stroll in privacy."

"An excellent suggestion." Charlie swept Grace to her feet. "Lead on, my love."

The path was delightfully secluded, but relatively little strolling was involved in their private moment together. Unfortunately, a group of walkers interrupted, and they had to move on in the interests of decorum. They headed in the opposite direction to the walkers, arm in arm, letting the tranquillity of the gardens flow over them.

"I had hoped we might spend a quiet few days together," Grace said. "Not that I am complaining, but we never seem to escape from the demands of work for long. I only hope our wedding day passes with no more drama than a petal or two dropped from the bouquets."

Charlie touched his fingers to the soft skin of her cheek. "I promise you, Grace Penrose, that nothing will stop me from exchanging marriage vows with you. Not even a horde of rampaging Vikings or a plague of locusts, let alone a petty criminal. As long as Jake doesn't speak up when the minister asks if anyone has a reason we should not be joined in holy matrimony, we will become man and wife in four weeks' time." He ran his fingers across her cheek and down her neck. "I wish it was sooner."

Grace laid her hands on top of his. "Fortunately, the risk of Vikings and locusts is low and my mother would strangle Jake if he spoke up, assuming I didn't get to him first. I am relieved to know that visiting my family hasn't put you off marrying me."

"On the contrary, it has been delightful seeing you all together and experiencing a Penrose Christmas. Any family that celebrates with a feast of thirteen desserts can be forgiven any other minor eccentricities, especially when they have been so ready to accept a lowly detective into their midst."

"They adore you, Charlie. My mother was of the firm opinion that no man would have me if I did not change my ways. She sees you as a miracle from heaven."

"Whereas your father has thanked me no less than three times for *not* making you change your ways. He is inordinately proud of you for training to become a doctor. As am I."

Grace had heard Charlie praise her vocation many times, but she never tired of it. Of course, he might think differently when he came to realise how inept she was at more traditional homemaking tasks, but somehow she didn't think so. "Shall we go home, Charlie? I want a good night's sleep before Christmas Eve, when Jake has his just deserts coming to him."

"Whereas I am very much looking forward to my just desserts – all thirteen of them."

Peace And Puddings

The Christmas Eve meal began at noon, to allow an entire afternoon and evening for digestion.

The Penrose family filed into the dining room with a degree of reverence appropriate for the feast awaiting them. A tablecloth of damask linen gleamed white under a mass of food – an enormous roast goose, glistening with crisp skin, a glazed ham, dishes of crunchy roast potatoes, honeyed carrots and yams, peas, and a gravy boat filled to the brim. Morsels wrapped in gold paper dotted the table, between twists of tinsel, silver candlesticks, place settings and crystal glasses.

Charlie took his seat next to his fiancée at the table, feeling very much part of the family. Mrs Penrose had been touched when Charlie offered to contribute a special dessert to the feast. When he confessed that it was part of his plan to get revenge on Jake, Mrs Penrose had chuckled gleefully and passed word to the rest of the family. Initial doubts that Jake would fall for the prank were dispelled when Charlie said he would pass off the pudding as a Chinese delicacy. In his experience, people would believe almost anything about a culture they were unfamiliar with.

The main course passed in peace and goodwill. Grace smiled a great deal and tried not to touch her ring, which was out of sight on a chain around her neck. Mrs Penrose was beaming with the knowledge that the wedding arrangements were in hand. Doctor Penrose was in fine spirits now that Durham House was saved. George was delighted that his microscope had helped solve a case. As for Peter and Paul, they needed only the feast to make them joyful.

Jake was the happiest of all of them. After those dreadful moments when he feared he might be implicated in a major crime, as an employee of Marton & Spragg, he was on top of the world. He had received praise from the police for uncovering the fraud and turning Mr Holliman in, and now he had a new business venture to look forward to. Jake had returned from his stroll with Martha Crockett that morning in a state of bliss. To top it off, Jake was sure Charlie had not yet found Grace's engagement ring.

Charlie smiled to himself, knowing Jake's triumph was premature. He held his plate out to Doctor Penrose, who carved slices of goose with the precision of a surgeon.

"I've never seen so much food in my life," Charlie whispered to Grace.

Grace raised an incredulous eyebrow. "This is nothing. The Christmas Eve feast is relatively restrained, to leave room for Christmas dinner with the extended family tomorrow."

"This is restrained?" Charlie whispered back.

"You'd better toughen up, Pyke, if you want to survive a Penrose Christmas. Those Scottish folks down south don't know what they're missing."

"The table looks beautiful," he said, for lack of a suitable reply.

"Grandma brought her French traditions with her," Grace explained. "Gold-wrapped sweets, three candlesticks, and a tablecloth knotted at the ends so the Devil can't get under the table. Papa has French wine brought into the country at great expense to honour his mother's heritage. That's what he says, anyway. If you ask me, he does it because he enjoys a nice vintage occasionally."

Mrs Penrose saved Charlie from replying. "Paul, please put those candlesticks back and say grace."

"I was looking for Grace's ring," Paul replied. "We ought to unwrap the sweets too, as they are exactly the kind of hiding place Jake would use." At the sight of his mother's face, Paul bowed his head and spoke the words of gratitude for the coming feast.

A period of hubbub followed as the carving knife was wielded, dishes were passed, glasses were clinked, napkin rings were rescued from the gravy, and groans of delight rippled up and down the table. Talk turned to the joys of the past year and hopes for the year to come, with Grace and Charlie's wedding at the top of everyone's minds.

Charlie noted Jake's amusement as Paul surreptitiously pressed the gold-wrapped treats to test for hard objects, while Paul fossicked in the tinsel and unknotted the tablecloth. Grace glanced at her unadorned ring finger and let out a soft sigh whenever she saw Jake was watching her.

Slowly but surely, they worked their way through the food, until the goose was down to the ribcage and the last roast potato was but a memory in a bloated belly. Charlie was looking forward to an hour or so of recuperation before the thirteen desserts came out.

"Well, this has been a jolly feast," Mrs Penrose said. "Who's ready for dessert?"

Charlie was staggered to hear cheers from the Penrose family, so soon after finishing the main course. He considered his own capacity for food to be far superior to any average-sized person, yet he would have begged for a rest break if he hadn't been determined to put a brave face on it.

"Don't look so worried, Charlie," Grace said. "Several of the thirteen desserts are lightweight affairs. Chocolates and nuts and dried fruits, for example."

"You are making light of a serious business, dear sister," George said, as he eased open the buttons of his waistcoat. "The yule log alone could sink a mortal man to the depths of the ocean if eaten in quantity. I still think that is where Jake has hidden your ring." George nudged Charlie in the ribs. "Grace holds the Penrose family record for the most slices of yule log eaten in one sitting. She set the record at the age of twelve and nobody has bested her since then. Perhaps Charlie could give it a go?"

120

"Not today, George." Charlie was already regretting the extra slice of goose Mrs Penrose had pressed on him. "I haven't had the years of practice that you have had."

Grace sat back and stifled a burp. "George is exaggerating my gluttony. Scraping the plate does not count as a whole slice and I had the smallest slice from the end too. Shall we bring the desserts in, Charlie? The activity might help to tamp down the main course to make some space."

Charlie eyed the row of desserts on the kitchen table, each more delicious that the last. His own creation was hidden in the larder, ready for him to bring out to the table last. When all the other dishes were on the table, he picked up his own wobbly white concoction and conveyed it to the table to oohs and ahhs. His pudding had come out far better than he had hoped, largely thanks to Aunt Sophie's artistry.

Charlie placed it in the only space left, which happened to be in front of Jake. His future brother-in-law stared in horror at the white blob, which was studded with round objects that looked startlingly like eyeballs.

"This is a special dessert from the Chinese side of my family," Charlie announced. "I am honoured that you are willing to include it in your feast. Indeed, I am honoured to be accepted into your family."

The family applauded, except Jake, who poked the pudding with his finger, causing it to wobble. "What is it?"

Mrs Penrose knocked his finger away. "Manners, Jake."

"It is made from sugar, gelatine and the eyeballs of fatted calves," Charlie said. "It is absolutely delicious, I assure you."

Jake's own eyeballs goggled at the monstrosity of a dessert in front of him, but the twins dug in with enthusiastic giggles. They fought over who got the most eyeballs, before stuffing heaped spoons into their mouths and groaning in delight.

Mrs Penrose took the dish, before the twins' antics upended it. She dished up a serving for George's wife, whose hands were full of little Georgie, and took a generous helping for herself.

"Mmm, delicious," Mrs Penrose said. "I've always loved trying recipes from other countries. Do you remember the food Lieutenant and Mrs Austin used to serve after they came home from India? Some of those curries could sizzle your eyeballs out of your sockets."

"Not half as good as this pudding," Doctor Penrose said, while digging in for another mouthful. "I do love the crunch of the eyeballs against the creamy texture of the calf-hoof gelatine. Delicious."

"We'll have to get Charlie to share more of his family recipes." George took a large helping, before shovelling a portion back. "Better save some for Jake and Charlie, before it's all gone." He passed the plate to Jake.

Jake eyed up the glutinous mass with horror. "You go right ahead, George. I'm saving myself for the yule log."

"Jake Penrose, don't you dare be discourteous," Grace hissed. "You'll give offence to Charlie's family."

Jake scooped the tiniest of eyeball-free slivers onto his plate.

Charlie reached over and scooped a giant blob of pudding onto Jake's plate, making sure to include several eyes. "No need to save any for me, Jake. I've eaten it a thousand times. You're going to love it. Don't be put off by the red streaks and the yellow stringy bits, it's only –"

"Stop!" Jake pushed the plate away. "I don't want to offend you, Charlie, but I simply cannot face it."

"Have you lost your appetite, dear?" his mother inquired. But the effort of keeping a straight face was too much for her. Mrs Penrose collapsed into tears of laughter, dragging the whole family with her.

Except Jake. He poked at his dessert. "You're teasing me, aren't you, Charlie? As if my blood relations weren't bad enough. I thought I could trust you. What is this, anyway?"

"Plain vanilla pudding," Charlie said. "With bulls-eye boiled sweets for decoration. Your Aunt Sophie had the brilliant idea of dipping them in white icing to cover most of the black, with a ring of food dye to make them look more like eyeballs."

George chuckled. "The master of trickery has been beaten at his own game,"

Paul and Peter pinged a pair of eyeballs at Jake, who ducked just in time.

Jake ate his dessert with good grace, managing a wan smile when teased. His good humour reemerged when Grace ordered George to cut the yule log into thin slices to ensure the hidden ring wasn't missed.

"Eat in small bites," Grace pleaded. "If anyone swallows my engagement ring, I'll make you clean it when it comes out the other end."

"Grace, not at the table," Doctor Penrose said, but only half-heartedly, as he was dissecting the profiteroles in search of sapphires.

Grace blew a kiss to Charlie while the others had their heads down, alternating between eating and guessing where the missing ring might be. Charlie sampled all thirteen desserts with relish, apparently with no ill effects. However, when the time came to rise from the table, Charlie had to push himself up with both arms and he swayed a little as he wiped his brow. Finally, she had found the limits of his appetite.

Grace helped Jake and the twins clear the table, noting that most of the desserts were only half eaten. They would reappear in subsequent days, until even the twins would declare that they didn't want to see another mille-feuille or cherry clafoutis ever again.

"Can we leave the washing up until later, my dear?" Doctor Penrose asked. "If my digestive tract doesn't have an hour or two to work uninterrupted, I may never recover."

Mrs Penrose patted his hand. "You say that every year, my dear, yet you're always cracking nuts and nibbling on leftovers before the afternoon is over."

The company retired to the drawing room. George and his father slumped into armchairs, groaning, while Charlie slouched on the sofa with his hand on his belly and his eyes half-closed.

Jake settled into his chair with a smug grin on his face. "Well, my dear family, the Christmas Eve feast is over for another year. I admit I deserved the pudding prank. I was wrong to question Charlie's abilities as a detective, after what he has achieved in so short a time since he arrived."

"Yes, bravo to Charlie and Grace," Doctor Penrose said, "for saving the orphans' home and unmasking a pair of rogues. Jake has a great deal to thank you two for."

"Wait, Father, I hadn't finished," Jake crowed. "They may be clever, but not clever enough to find Grace's ring. It's time to hand over grandfather's watch, Grace."

"Give me back my ring first," Grace demanded.

Christmas Carols

Jake strutted over to the nativity scene and reached to the back of the stable. He felt around for a few seconds, without success. "It's right here ..." Jake pulled out all the figurines and tried again. "Just a moment ..." All traces of cockiness had seeped away.

The manger, the animal stalls, and a scattering of straw followed the figurines, until the stable was a bare shell. But still Jake was empty-handed when he turned back to his captivated audience. "The ring seems to have got stuck under the floor of the stable," Jake said with a light laugh, which held more panic than amusement. "I jammed the ring in with a wad of brown felt to save it from being scratched."

"Jake Penrose," his mother said sternly, "how in the name of all the saints was Charlie supposed to find the ring wrapped and hidden underneath the floor of the stable?"

"Unsporting, indeed," Doctor Penrose admonished.

Jake picked up the stable and shook it.

"Don't you dare, Jake," his mother cried. "It's bad enough that you prised up the floor without destroying the entire structure."

"The floor was already loose," Jake said. "I only lifted it a little more."

"Jake, stop tormenting me." Grace's words came out in a shrill sob. "I want my ring back."

Jake paled at the sight of welling tears in his sister's eyes. "Grace, I'm sorry. The ring must have been knocked further into the gap underneath. Don't cry, please. I'll get it out."

Charlie handed him a pencil as a probe. "You had better find it, Jake," he said, with a tremor in his voice. "That ring was made by a craftsman jeweller who is no longer alive. I have seen no other ring that comes close to its perfection."

Jake's fingers trembled as he poked under the gap in the floor with the pencil, but the nativity scene was not giving up any secrets. "Grace, I don't know what to say. I'm going to have to break it open."

"You'll do no such thing," his mother declared. "It is a family heirloom. Your grandmother would turn in her grave."

Jake didn't know who to look at or what to do.

Grace took pity on him. "Looking for this, Jake?"

She fluttered her hand in front of her brother to show off the sapphire and diamond ring she had slipped onto her finger while Jake was distracted. "Charlie solved your little mystery in a trice. Did you not notice that I have been wearing the ring around my neck all this while?"

Jake stared at the ring, then switched his disbelieving gaze to Charlie. His cheeks turned as red as the cherries they had feasted on for dessert.

Charlie gave a modest shrug. "Detecting is my job, after all."

The rest of the family was having none of it. Those who weren't laughing were slapping Charlie on the back or prodding Jake in the ribs.

Jake held up his hands in surrender. "I concede defeat. Congratulations, Charlie, you have not only survived your first Penrose Christmas Eve feast, you have proved yourself worthy of my sister." Jake went to the mantlepiece, where he had left the prize. He handed the music box to Grace with a bow and a flourish. "I hope I won't be reminded of this moment for the rest of my life."

"You can count on it," Grace replied, as she wound the key and opened the lid, started the tinkle of music. "I could listen to it over and over and over again."

126

"I never liked that music box anyway," Jake grumbled. "I don't know why Grandma Penrose gave it to me, when Grace got the watch."

"It's beautiful, Jake. A family treasure."

"A music box is not the right gift for a young lad, Grace. Grandpa's watch was more … well, manly. I'm happy for you to have the music box if you like it. The bare spot on my shelf will be a constant reminder to be humble." Jake gave a rueful shrug. "Grandma told me that if I took the time to appreciate her gift, it would bring me good luck. She got that wrong."

"Not all treasures have a monetary value, Jake," Mrs Penrose said.

Charlie picked up the music box and examined it. "It's heavier than one might expect. And thicker than the mechanism warrants." He turned it over in his hands, peering closely, with the help of the magnifying lens he kept in his notebook.

After a few false starts, the bottom of the box opened at his touch, revealing a dozen gold coins. Jake let out a whimper.

"I haven't seen this type of coin before." Charlie passed one to Doctor Penrose.

"St George and the Dragon sovereigns, from before Queen Victoria's reign," Doctor Penrose said. "Well, I never. My mother brought gold coins to New Zealand after selling her rare book collection in England before she sailed. Your grandmother was right, after all, Jake. You would have been well rewarded if you had only taken the time to appreciate her gift."

Jake was speechless.

His mother consoled him with a pat on the shoulder. "How nice that Grace and Charlie have such a generous gift from you to begin their life together. I wouldn't put it past your grandma to have intended it as a lesson for you all along."

Charlie upended the music box and held out the coins to Jake. "We can't take these, Jake. Your grandmother intended the money to go to you. She would have been proud to see you starting your own business."

Jake's hand hovered, but he pulled it back. "Take the coins, Charlie. You and Grace have earned them. Without you two, I would be facing Christmas as a much poorer man. In fact, if Spragg had disappeared without a trace, as he intended, I might be facing charges of conspiring to defraud our clients, rather than pocketing extra wages."

Grace took the music box and gold sovereigns from Charlie. She ruffled her brother's hair. "You have the makings of a fine brother in you, Jake. I expect I haven't made your life easy in the past, but there's a new year ahead for us both. Shall we call a truce?"

"Agreed," Jake replied, "especially now that it is two against one. Now take that darned music box away before I change my mind, and don't expect a lavish wedding present."

When Grace came back a few minutes later, the family was crowded around the window, watching a group of carol singers coming up the street. Grace slipped a newly wrapped present under the Christmas tree and went to join them. Jake was first to the door as the carollers came in the gate. The rest of the family formed a semi-circle around him on the veranda.

Grace understood Jake's uncharacteristic eagerness to listen to carols once she realised it was the orphans' choir, with Martha and the choirmaster singing at the back of the group. Eva was at the front, her arms linked with the girl beside her, with Tom on her other side. Eva and Tom gave a little wave when they recognised Charlie and Grace.

When the choir finished singing two verses of "Silent Night", Jake invited them all into the drawing room. Mrs Penrose bustled around, handing out hot fruit punch, minus the sherry. Jake and the twins disappeared into the kitchen and returned with plates and desserts for the children and coins for the collection box.

Martha joined Grace and Charlie by the Christmas tree. "I wanted to thank you again for all you have done for my family. And Doctor

Penrose too, who has been generous in offering his services to fix Tom's twisted foot."

"Tom and Eva are terrific children," Charlie said. "I'm glad they have found a loving home."

"We have a lot to be thankful for this Christmas," Martha said. "Durham House is secure, with Mr Waterstone showing every sign of being a generous patron to our cause. And, most wonderful of all, my family has a better life to look forward to, thanks to you and Mr Waterstone."

"We're glad, Martha," Grace said. "I hope Eva will not be scared of her new home."

"Oh no, not at all. I explained to Eva that what she saw in Mr Spragg's house was nothing more than statues. She and Tom thought it hilarious and insisted on seeing the house straight away. Mr Spragg was outside, in a cart piled with trunks. It was a strange thing to witness. One might have thought he would be miserable, but Mr Spragg looked as if a weight had been lifted off his shoulders. He looked as excited as a child receiving a much longed-for Christmas present."

Grace noticed Jake gazing wistfully in their direction. "Talking of Christmas presents, we have gifts for Eva and Tom. Why don't you sit by Jake while I get them?"

Jake stood up as Martha approached. His eyes didn't leave her as he invited her to sit beside him. The only person who looked happier was Mrs Penrose, who exchanged a conspiratorial wink with her daughter.

Grace picked up three presents, handing one to Jake. "Are you going to give Martha the present you got her, Jake?" She had to give his foot a nudge with her boot before he came out of his trance and passed on the gift.

Martha unwrapped the gold paper, revealing the music box. "Oh, how lovely."

"It originally belonged to Jake's grandmother," Grace said. "Grandma always said it would bring him good luck, didn't she Jake? She was never wrong."

"I hope you like it, Miss Crockett," Jake mumbled belatedly. Blushing mightily, he reached over to open the box and start the music. "I know how you much you enjoy music."

Martha's cheeks were equally rosy as she listened to the tune and smiled at Jake. "It is the most beautiful gift I have ever received. I shall treasure it always, Mr Penrose."

Mission accomplished, Grace went back to Charlie, who had gathered Tom and Eva around him. "We bought a Christmas gift for each of you too, to welcome you to Wellington."

Tom ripped the paper from his present, scattering the gold-wrapped sweets Grace had put in with the small magnifying glass she had found in Kirkcaldie & Stains. Eva nudged her brother, who was gazing at the present in puzzled delight. "Thank you," Tom said. "What is it?"

"Detectives use magnifying glasses to see clues close up," Charlie explained. He showed Tom, who proceeded to examine every object within reach. The sweets lay untouched as Tom became engrossed in studying a dead fly the twins kindly pointed out on a windowsill, to Mrs Penrose's horror.

Eva opened her present with great care, to avoid ripping the paper. "A book of carols! Thank you, Miss Penrose. It's wonderful. May I show it to my friend?"

"Of course, Eva." Grace was sure she felt the warmth of her grandmother's touch on her shoulder as she watched the festive scene. Grace turned to find the touch was Charlie's hand. He bent his head to hers, but they needed no words to express their satisfaction with the turn of events this Christmas Eve.

The older members of the choir gathered up the plates, emptied down to the last crumb and lick of cream, and thanked the Penrose family for their welcome. Martha left the music box with Jake, who promised to return it to her tomorrow.

Once the carollers had left, the Penrose family sank into their chairs with sighs of contentment, wondering if perhaps there might be just a little space in their stomachs for a chocolate or two.

Only Jake was restless. "It seems I am in your debt yet again, Grace, for gaining me Miss Crockett's favour. And don't try to pretend that the music box was Grandma Penrose's grand plan to bring me happiness from beyond the grave."

"Merely a nudge in the right direction, brother," Grace said. "I didn't have to have Grandma Penrose's powers of perception to realise you and Martha admired each other."

"You are underestimating your grandmother's foresight, Jake," Charlie said. "I would never have found the ring if it hadn't been for her."

"How did you find the ring, Charlie?" Doctor Penrose asked. "Especially when Jake went to such lengths to conceal it."

Mrs Penrose wagged a finger at Jake. "And if you even think of pulling any pranks at Grace and Charlie's wedding, I will make your every living minute a misery for the rest of your life."

"Not a chance, Mother," Jake replied. "I have learned my lesson. Do tell us, Charlie, how did you find the ring?"

"Jake told me to look for something Grace loved about Christmas. For all the teasing she gets over the Christmas desserts, I know what Grace loves most are the family traditions passed down by her grandmother."

"Quite so," Grace agreed.

Charlie rummaged under the Christmas tree. "Grace recalled the tune to her grandmother's favourite French carol, and I felt sure I was on the right track when I dreamed about her grandmother singing the carol." Charlie handed the parcel to Grace. "I thought you might like a copy as a present. Aunt Sophie provided the words, Peter acted as scribe, Paul illustrated the border, and the pair of them found a frame to put it in."

Grace tore the paper in her haste. "Exquisite! What a wonderful present. Thank you Charlie, and you too, Peter and Paul. I've never seen the carol written in English." Grace read the words of the carol to her family.

"Between the ox and the grey donkey
Sleep, sleep, sleep the little son
A thousand divine angels, a thousand seraphim
fly around this great god of love.

Between the two arms of Mary
Sleep, sleep, sleep the fruit of life
A thousand divine angels, a thousand seraphim
fly around this great god of love.

Between roses and lilies
Sleep, sleep, sleep the little son
A thousand divine angels, a thousand seraphim
fly around this great god of love.

Between the pretty shepherds
Sleep, sleep, Jesus smiling
A thousand divine angels, a thousand seraphim
fly around this great god of love.

On this beautiful day so solemn
Sleep, sleep, sleep Emmanuel
A thousand divine angels, a thousand seraphim
fly around this great god of love."

"It's called 'Between the Ox and the Grey Donkey'," Charlie said. "The carol matches the nativity scene, so I searched between the ox and the donkey and felt a slight bump in the floor of the stable. Simple."

"Simple?" George spluttered. "Impossibly devious, if you ask me. Why did you make it so hard, Jake?"

Jake shrugged. "I thought it would teach Grace a lesson. Surely I wasn't the only one tired of having the ring waved in my face, with Grace going on and on about what a wonderful man and exceptional detective her fiancé is?"

Grace spluttered. "Would you prefer I told everyone that Charlie is a plain, dull, untalented person, like Martha Crockett?"

Jake rose from his seat, his chest puffed out and his cheeks pink. "Grace Penrose, how dare you suggest that Martha Crockett is plain and untalented. She is a vision of all that is good and wonderful."

Jake's flare of annoyance deflated at the amusement of his family. "Oh, yes, well, I see that I have underestimated the power of love to render a person foolish. I concede defeat in every possible way." He waited for the laughter to die down. "If you will excuse me, I have a sudden desire to hear more Christmas carols."

He strode to the door, stopping at the threshold. "You're wrong though, Charlie. My choice of hiding place had nothing to do with Grandma or her French carol, which I hadn't even remembered until you reminded us of it. You found the ring by blind chance, nothing more."

The door banged behind him. A whistled version of "Good King Wenceslas" faded up the street.

Grace settled onto the sofa beside her fiancé. "He'll never learn, will he? Call it intuition or exceptional detective skills, but blind chance it was not."

"I have to admit it wasn't entirely due to our very own Ghost of Christmas Past, in the form of your grandmother," Charlie said. "Jake was the first to give the game away. He has a habit of flaring his nostrils slightly when he is anxious. While you were all searching the room to find the missing ring, I watched Jake. The only time he flared his nostrils was when the twins inspected the nativity scene. I thought I was wrong when the twins didn't find the ring, but the dream and the words of the carol made me take a closer look. But don't tell Jake that, because I wouldn't want him to think it was easy."

"He certainly won't hear it from me." Grace chuckled. "Solving a mystery is a bit like magic, isn't it? Easy when you know how it is done, perplexing if you don't."

"I think we've had quite enough mystery for one Christmas," Mrs Penrose said. "Could I interest you in another slice of yule log, Charlie dearest?"

"Now you mention it, Mrs Penrose, I do believe I could manage a sliver. After that, perhaps we might hear the rest of Dickens' story? I'm eager to hear how the tale ends."

Paul jumped up to get the yule log, while Peter gaped at Charlie. "You must know the story, Charlie. The wicked old miser, Scrooge, learns to be kind and charitable, while poor little Tiny Tim is saved."

"Charlie was teasing, Peter." Grace rested her head in her favourite spot beside her fiancé's shoulder. "Everyone knows how *A Christmas Carol* ends."

"Happily ever after, as every story ought to end." Mrs Penrose sipped her punch and beamed a contented smile on her nearest and dearest, saving an extra twinkle for her future son-in-law.

134

Read on

In Book 6 of the Penrose and Pyke Mystery series, *Murder Ignited*, Grace and Charlie's wedding day is thrown into chaos, after a protest at Lavender House sparks a fatal fire.

If you wish to know more about Grace's grandmother, I invite you to read my previous series of books, the **French Legacy Trilogy**.

Thank You

Thank you for reading this story. If you enjoyed it, I would be very grateful if you would leave a rating or review to help other readers discover it.

Find out about other books and sign up for notifications of new releases at https://RosePascoe.com

Historical Notes

A nod to Charles Dickens, whose most famous Christmas novella has been inspiring readers for generations. The release of *A Christmas Carol* in December 1843 sparked a wave of charitable giving and a new level of enthusiasm for celebrating Christmas with family gatherings and feasts.

The popularity of Christmas, including decorated Christmas trees and cards, had already been growing in England, after being introduced from Germany by Queen Victoria's husband and other royal relatives. The Christmas carol "Silent Night" was composed in 1818, but popularised in Britain during Victoria's reign, as were other Christmas traditions. Tinsel had been around since the sixteenth century and was added to the Victorian Christmas tree to add sparkle to the candlelight.

In my story, Grace's French grandmother had a strong influence on the Penrose family celebrations. Christmas Eve was a time for French families to celebrate with a feast. The tradition of having thirteen desserts is a regional one, which I have appropriated for the sake of the story because it was too delicious to leave out. The French Christmas carol featured in this story, *"Entre le bœuf et l'âne gris"* ("Between the ox and the grey donkey"), is said to be one of the oldest carols, dating back at least five centuries.

The orphans' home and all characters in this story are fictional.

www.ingramcontent.com/pod-product-compliance
Lightning Source LLC
Chambersburg PA
CBHW010936120626
46554CB00007B/2490